M000284710

Praise for *Exhibit*

"In prose at once sharp and lush, Kwon crafts a gripping tale of a woman wrestling with the past, while boldly making her own future. A haunting and powerful exploration of art, racism, feminism, and desire, this novel will stay with me a long time."

—Madeline Miller, *New York Times* bestselling author of *Circe* and *The Song of Achilles*

"*Exhibit* is sensational—a novel that's both intimate and operatic, singular and world-encompassing. Kwon's prose is soulful and piercing, chronicling the many ways we lose and find ourselves, blending love and sex and fables between the infinite folds that encompass desire. *Exhibit* is entirely captivating, and Kwon is truly masterful; it's a book for the mind and the heart and the body, an actual tour de force."   —Bryan Washington, bestselling author of *Family Meal* and *Memorial*

"*Exhibit* is extraordinary: brisk, jolting, brilliant, beautiful, true. A ghost story, a tale of passion, a captivating portrait of how art is made, it turns myths upside down, assumptions inside out, all in the most exquisite prose in the bookstore. Kwon is one of the finest American writers, and her latest is a must for all readers."

—Andrew Sean Greer, Pulitzer Prize–winning author of *Less Is Lost*

"I tore through this. *Exhibit* explores how obliteration can be a kind of rebirth, how the nuances of that are complicated by the constraints of chosen and socially imposed identities. Kwon writes about art and ardor with urgency."

—Raven Leilani, *New York Times* bestselling author of *Luster*

"A rare jewel of a book, at once forceful and unrepentant, delicate and shimmering. R. O. Kwon carves language into a wondrous, jagged thing, revealing facets of desire usually hidden. To read *Exhibit* is to feel time slow down."

—C Pam Zhang, bestselling author of *How Much of These Hills Is Gold* and *Land of Milk and Honey*

EXHIBIT

Also by R. O. Kwon

The Incendiaries

Also Edited by R. O. Kwon

Kink

EXHIBIT

R. O. KWON

권오경

RIVERHEAD BOOKS

NEW YORK

2024

RIVERHEAD BOOKS
An imprint of Penguin Random House LLC
penguinrandomhouse.com

Copyright © 2024 by R. O. Kwon
Penguin Random House supports copyright. Copyright fuels creativity,
encourages diverse voices, promotes free speech, and creates a vibrant culture.
Thank you for buying an authorized edition of this book and for complying with
copyright laws by not reproducing, scanning, or distributing any part of it in
any form without permission. You are supporting writers and allowing
Penguin Random House to continue to publish books for every reader.

Riverhead and the R colophon are registered
trademarks of Penguin Random House LLC.

Library of Congress Cataloging-in-Publication Data

Names: Kwon, R. O., author.
Title: Exhibit / R. O. Kwon.
Description: First edition. | New York: Riverhead Books, 2024. |
Includes bibliographical references.
Identifiers: LCCN 2023027686 (print) | LCCN 2023027687 (ebook) |
ISBN 9780593190029 (hardcover) | ISBN 9780593190043 (ebook)
Subjects: LCGFT: Novels.
Classification: LCC PS3611.W68 E94 2024 (print) |
LCC PS3611.W68 (ebook) | DDC 813/.6—dc23/eng/20230615
LC record available at https://lccn.loc.gov/2023027686
LC ebook record available at https://lccn.loc.gov/2023027687

Printed in the United States of America
1st Printing

Book design by Alexis Farabaugh

This is a work of fiction. Names, characters, places,
and incidents either are the product of the author's imagination or are
used fictitiously, and any resemblance to actual persons, living or dead,
businesses, companies, events, or locales is entirely coincidental.

To people kept out of the record

이책은 기록되지 않은 사람들에게 바칩니다

Am I a monster or is this
what it means to be human?

.

Clarice Lispector, *The Hour of the Star*

EXHIBIT

1.

She'd go up the tall pine first. He flung his leg on a bough, close behind. She didn't slip, her leaps agile. Hanbok silk, bright, swift, flared with each jump. If cloth tangled with a sprig, he lunged to help. In the fresh light, they kept going, as high as possible.

His parents, upset, hadn't slept. He'd spoken, the past night, of his plan to wed a kisaeng. Startled, his parents said he must be joking. No kisaeng, paid to sing, jig, and flirt in public, had the right to wed a Han. Not just a Han, the prized first son, obliged to pass along his line. He'd beg pardon, then forget this whore of a girl.

Instead, as I told Lidija, he replied that he loved this kisaeng. She'd be his wife. If you don't stop talking, his father said, I'll kill you. Lips tight, the son left. Night lifted. Oil-polished hanji doors slid open; a maid wailed. Paired bodies hung from the pine, hanboks rippling. Necks breaking, they'd died.

In my 엄마's telling, this old tale proved lasting, trailing bodies, spoiled lives, and evil I'd also, perhaps, inherit. People said the kisaeng's spirit, abiding, hostile to all Hans, kept us cursed. It might be nothing. But spite held a ghost close to the living. It was best, though, not to talk of this spirit. I ought to tell future offspring, a husband. "No one else, darling," 엄마 said. Just by talking, I'd rustle up the kisaeng's ghost.

Still, it might find me, this birthright evil. I'd flag it through a wild urge: to risk, for a futile, single love, all the ties I rated high. I had to kill this longing. If I didn't, I'd light my life on fire.

•

I said I'd listen. For a while, I did. But that June night in Marin, with Lidija, I felt this pledge's hold, like hexed rope, shred, rip, then fall. Philip, you'll ask how I told this person I'd just met what I kept from you. I've tried figuring it out, sifting the burnt pile of all that I ignited. It's true that, with Lidija, I let go of rules by which I'd lived. Not long after the night in Marin, she fixed a gag to my face. It was big. Spit-wet, the globe fell out. Lidija, impatient, applied foil tape. It stayed on, but left the skin she'd taped shining red. I had a rash, allergic.

I told Philip I'd reacted to a lip balm. But if not for the lying,

I'd have loved this rash; I forgot to be vain. It was put up like a sign, as though I might be hers.

·

I'd refused, at first, to go to Marin for the night. It was a shindig hosted by Irving Noth, a friend of Philip. Irving was sitting a friend's place.

"He invited you," I said, to Philip.

"But you're also Irving's friend," he said.

"Irving isn't a friend."

"His rival, then."

"Oh, *no*," I said, jolted. It was a fresh shock, the earth tilting again. Until this past month, I didn't think Philip, of all people, might be capable of knowing me so little. But his smile, furling, let slip the joke. I laughed, then Philip did, too, relieved. I'd avoided Irving since graduate school. I'd judged him to be a child, his art slapdash. None of this made Irving a rival. For him to be eligible, I had to respect his work.

Philip might spend the night, in Marin. But, I said: the 8 a.m. flight. St. Paul, a friend's wedding. Of course, Philip said. He'd pack all the bags. If we spent the night, we'd go right from Marin to the airport.

"Jin, I want you with me," he said. Philip insisted; fine, I said, I'd go. His face broke open, jubilant. In the car, we kept quiet. Dazed, I thought, still new to this upturn in fighting. I'd argued with Philip for hours. He parked along a hilltop incline; the wind gusting, I held Philip's hand. On the bridge's far side, haze ringed pale buildings. But here, I didn't taste ash from the fires up north. I asked if Philip noticed the shift. He nodded, pulling in a long, full breath before he rang the bell.

Irving flung the door open. "Philip! Jin, hello! You're the first people here." In the kitchen, he filled highballs as he spoke of friends he expected. Sculptors, artists: who else? I forget; the spotlight circling Lidija unrolls, this large halo, glaring like a path to the sun. I've lost what else he said until I heard of Lidija.

"Not Lydia," he said, sliding us drinks. "L-i-d-i-j-a, Lidija Jung. It's a spelling she picked, at the ripe age of five, after she started taking ballet lessons. With the hope of being a little more Slavic, like the dancers Lidija idolized. *Five*. Isn't that wild?"

"Is that what she does?" I asked. "She dances?"

"She's injured, but yes."

"Did she quit?"

"No, but she can't perform again until her leg's fixed." Lidija lived in New York, he said. Did Philip and I often go to the ballet? Oh, well, if we had a chance to watch Lidija's dancing, we should. "Lidija's rising so fast that she skipped the corps to be a soloist. She's a principal, at ballet's height. She has this fabled jump, light, floating, as though she's levitating. Ballet legend has it that, in class, while she leapt, Lidija was told, 'Stay up high.' For an instant, she did."

I glanced at Irving. Not taking pride, as I'd expect, in this guest. No, I thought, elated, like a herald with glad tidings: lo, the miracle is nigh. I, too, hoped to see this Lidija dancing. I asked how they'd met.

"Last July, at a ballet festival."

Irving spoke about the festival; I put a hand on Philip's back. I thought of the day's fight. It wasn't long ago that, while agitated, I'd lie on top of Philip. If I'd ride the lifting, falling of his chest, I might find calm. But, at last, not even Philip could help.

•

"*Both* of you don't want children?" friends used to ask.

"No," Philip and I said.

"If one of you changes your mind, though—"

"Oh, but we won't."

•

The bell rang. Irving's guests jostled through. People dived in the pool. No sign of Lidija. Philip changed into trefoil-printed shorts I'd bought with him in Seoul. He'd joined me at the end of a six-week post-college teaching job. It was hot; Philip hadn't packed a bathing suit. In Seoul, clothing ran small. "Pick those," I told him, while he tried on ill-fitting shorts in blithe, parading colors, the tight fabric vivid with jade, topaz, fire opal, brushed gold. I said to get them all; I loved the sight of him. For all I'd travel, since then, working, I hadn't left Philip behind that long again.

"No, wait," I told Philip. He'd shed his shirt; I had sun lotion in a handbag. I applied it to Philip's back, milk fluid spilling to his hips. "Here you go," I said, with a final pat. "You're safe."

In the shade of a large hat, I sat on the pool's lip. Philip held my legs. "I burn fast," I said, to people asking when I'd get in. Moving the hat's angle, I shaded Philip, too. Strips of light rippled then slashed open, limbs flailing through bright ribbons. Partiers floated up to us, a couple of Irving's friends.

"You're Jin Han, right?" One was Quin; one, Elijah. Both sculpted, and loved the photo triptychs I'd shown last June, in New York. Quin still had the catalog. She did, Elijah said. Quin kept the catalog out, flat, open, on a side table. I asked if they'd tell me about their work; after a while, I had the sculptors laughing. I hosted an ongoing pub gathering for local artists, I said. Drinks, informal, just for talking. Did the sculptors wish to come? Oh, yes.

Quin and Elijah left. Philip said he'd take part in a game of Marco Polo; I went inside.

•

Philip, a month ago, had woken up desiring a child. I still didn't, as I'd told Philip, often, from the time we'd started dating. Philip had felt as I did. But this novel urge kept him in its grip. Holding a friend's infant, he'd put his face to the child's head, inhaling. "It's the scent," Philip said, baffled. His friend, chortling, had replied, Oh, so it begins. Philip lusted to clasp his own child. He pined for the infant's weight in his arms. Not a scrap of me did. Philip, I hadn't said it out loud, but for the first time, it felt possible this split, a single rip, might pull us apart.

•

It was quiet in the Marin house. I didn't let a night end until I'd taken photos. It was the fiat ruling my life, a ritual I'd upheld since college. But I also, since last June, hadn't shot a picture worth saving. I taught a class; I had a reviewing gig. With no photos to sell, I'd be obliged to go back to the bar job I'd held until last June. It paid well enough, in tips; I'd quit the instant I could. Plus, six months ago, invited to join a high-profile group exhibition, I'd said yes. I had to finish the images by this fall. But I'd get a drink, I thought. One julep, then I'd take pictures.

I got out the gin julep supplies Philip and I had brought. I put ice in a dishrag; glass panels slid wide.

"You're Lidija," I said. Shining from a dip in the pool: Lidija, martial. She had long, taut posture, a neck rising tall. Upon its height, she lifted her head like a flag. I knew, at first sight, who she had to be.

"I am," she said, turning. It didn't surprise Lidija, being noticed.

"Irving talked about a dancer named Lidija Jung," I said. "I'm Jin."

Lidija eyed the julep supplies I'd set out. "Not going in the pool?"

"Maybe later," I said.

With a one-sided shrug, she picked up sun lotion. She bent her head; dyed pale, Lidija's crown radiated light. Would Lidija's birth name be Lydia, or Lidia? Jung might be Korean; I hadn't met a lot of Korean people named Lydia. Lisa, perhaps. Elise. Lillian. "The last time I was in a pool, I burned," Lidija said. "I flaked skin. I had fish scales in my clothing."

"Can I fix you a drink?"

"No, thank you."

I had nothing else to ask. She applied lotion in thick piles. Lidija had ink, a line of script, coiling up from the striped wrap she'd slung on her hips. It was illegible, veiled in white liquid. I had to figure out what it said. She tipped lotion down the slope of a ridged leg. I rinsed a highball, trying not to watch. Lidija's film of lotion hid while inviting, flashing what it kept back. Injured, Lidija moved as if foreign to pain.

I was used to this pull, though, Philip. It was a lifelong allure, the gloss of a bold, strong girl. I hit the ice with a rolling pin, to crack it. She'd baptized herself, at five, with a ballet stage name. It was striking, a thrill, Lidija's brio as she applied lotion, not caring if I'd watch. But I just, I thought, studied to learn.

"Still no pool?" Lidija asked.

"In a minute."

"I don't believe you," she said. With a laugh, she glided out.

•

I filled a pitcher with juleps; Irving's friends swept in. People lingered, talking, then left, juleps in hand. Silence rang, abrupt. I had time alone, but not for long. Irving had spoken of a turret I might like. On the third level, he'd said. I hoisted my bag.

Julep finished, I began to go up the stairs. I'd spent half a decade on the images I'd shown last June. It was a solo exhibition of large-scale triptychs. For a while, I'd lived in fanatic pursuit of relics. Mirific pilgrim sites. Signs of the alleged divine. I applied for stipends that paid for trips to Lourdes, to Spain, fresh Christ sightings in El Paso, Irvine, and Philadelphia. In situ, I shot faded twists of cloth, ash-pile Marian leavings. Bits of antique flesh. Reputed marvels.

I'd plotted, as a child, to give my life to the Lord. In college, I'd lost this faith. Isolated, grief-wild, I'd picked through ruins He'd left behind. If I could still love this orphan world, deprived of His salvific light, which parts of it might even I, broken as I came, find worth prizing?

In this exile, I'd relied on photos, image. I shot in full-frame digital; I aspired to rich, opulent hues. I required solid detail. But chasing fabled signs of Christ, I shot pale wisps, the objects insipid. Images proved dull, harsh. I had nothing until, in line at a Michigan church, salt ice hissing with pilgrims' steps, plumes rising through vivid lips, I noticed the living bodies. People, not relics, I thought, at which point the images began rioting to life.

.

Faint, shifting colors led to Irving's turret. It was a high-walled hexagon. Prism light fell through oriel glass. Its ceiling arched. I heard partiers' talk flitting in; I added a telephoto lens to the camera I'd brought. Nudging open an oriel, I rested on its sill.

Outside, Philip lined up with five people, holding the tile edge, then exploded forward, racing. Lidija had gone in. Philip fell behind; laughing, he stopped. He flipped down. I slowed my breath, taking a shot of him. His legs kicked, Icarian; I shot again. Foliage stirred, rustling. One shot, then I changed the lens. In public, if asked, I said I'd depend on habit, on pattern. I didn't skip a day's work, I told people. Not for anything. I tried a wide-angled fourth shot. I still didn't, taking short-lived images as though I put hope in the act. Fifth picture; the sixth. I adjusted the focus. One final shot of Philip. I staged the ritual, like a doubt-riddled priest clad in his slipping faith.

If, for Philip's sake, I gave in to a milk-bathed life I didn't want—

But I'm not giving in, I thought. I flicked through shots. Nothing, again. I had a friend, Elise Liu, who kept all photos intact, filed. But I'd kill a bad image, each inept shot the sign of a one-hit fraud. Not the kind of work I did, images of people racing. In the past, I'd started with a guiding plan. Of late, though, I flailed. I tried anything, with no idea of what I was doing. I got rid of the images; I left the turret. Hurtling down the stairs, I heard rattling, then a door opened. Quin stepped out.

I began saying hello; I faltered. Quin was crying.

"Can you tell Irving I had to go?" she asked.

I'd tell Irving, I said. "Did you drive? If not, can I help call you a car, or—"

"No, Elijah's driving. Is Ralph Hill a friend of yours?"

"Who?"

"He's tall, white," Quin said. "He just arrived. Jin, I'm urging you to avoid Ralph. Don't tell Irving. It's not that, he isn't, Irving didn't do anything. But I just met Irving a night ago. You can tell Lidija, though. Lidija Jung. It's up to you."

●

I noted, outside, a tall person who had to be this Ralph. Still clothed, a late arrival, in Madras plaid. Quin had told me to avoid Ralph since, like Quin, I was Asian. She'd made this plain, isolating Lidija, the third Asian person at Irving's. It leapt past tallying, the life total of alerts from girls, women, advising, Listen, be careful. Lidija reclined in a patio chair, legs tucked. "Jin," Philip called. I'd tell Lidija when I could.

Irving's friends traipsed in, flushed. He passed along a dish of pills, the sun rolling out of sight. I idled with a group in the living room, skittish, unsure of the pills. But then, I let in a breath to open wide, unfurling large, full. Music whirled its spun gold, a radiant spiral. Eluding its coil, I slid out, alone.

I bathed my legs in vast liquid. Its surface flexed, a live jewel, lit a vital, elating blue. Images refused the will. But if I pled, if I kept calling, they'd listen, perhaps. What did I do to fail you? I asked. I stirred pale fingers through lapis-blue, trailing stars. It was quiet; after a while, I went in, to Philip.

He sat on kitchen tiles with Irving. Philip asked how I was doing; I rested a palm on top of his head. Philip's soft, fine strands. If I told him I'd like to talk, he'd jump up. He'd run to help. Philip and I, we had to end this fight dividing us.

"Will you come find me?" I asked. Philip said he would.

I walked in the living room. Lidija sprawled on a couch, limbs out. She sat up. "It's you," she said; we began talking. Others tried joining us, then left. Lidija's pupils held flecks of goldfoil light. She asked how I'd met Philip.

"In college, at Edwards," I said. Until Philip, I'd had late-night flings at college parties, on thin futons. Quick spins with a half-dozen women, along with a couple of men. But Philip was the first person I'd dated, and the last. I'd wed Philip, then we left New York, for his job.

Lidija asked about the wedding. Philip and I held it on the college lawn. Paper lanterns filled the courtyard with felled suns. It was July, the heat thick, soft. I thought I might float on the night; I kept a hand tethered on Philip's arm. Most guests stayed out late, reveling. One guest woke on the Edwards lawn, gown dew-spoiled, legs twined with a stranger's. But Philip and I walked to the hotel, wishing to be alone again. I toted white stilettos, ill-used soles aching; I had to stop at a bench, to sit. It was by the chapel. Philip tried the doors. Finding the place open, we christened a stall. Its prie-dieu, the hard, pushing edge, hostile to a silk-clad spine. If it hurt, I didn't care. I hoped to profane.

Night rushed along. Lidija said, "Let's go to the patio chairs."

Outside, I dipped a shawl in twists of light. Netting rippled, drifting; I'd fish up the liquid stars.

"How do you fill your time?" Lidija said.

"Is this your way of asking what I do?"

"It is."

"I take pictures," I said.

"You take—as in, you're an artist?"

"Yes."

"What's your last name?"

"Han. Irving said you live in New York."

"I'm here for a while," Lidija said. "I'm injured, so I'm losing time. But I have drills. Physical therapists. I'm also trying to learn to choreograph. It begins in a month, the workshop. I'll go back after that. I have to ask you, though, Jin. Will you take my picture tonight?"

"Oh, no. I can't. It won't be right."

"Let's try, though."

I didn't protest again. She'd go to New York. I did want a shot; I said I'd be back. Fetching the bag, I went to Lidija, who'd hauled patio chairs to a lamp spilling mild, white light. Stars pricked the evening. I tried a quick shot of Lidija's angled face.

"Why'd you start with saying no?" Lidija asked, a fist to her chin.

"Hold still."

Nerves fired, alerting me to this instant I couldn't let slip. Lidija's head, swept with light. Notice this, I thought, skin flickering. Bold obliques of Lidija's clavicles, raised as if taking flight. But I was high; Lidija glinted at the edges, fine sparks igniting.

"I didn't bring a tripod," I said. "Plus, high, I have lying sight. I'm gilding the image."

"I had my head dyed."

"I figured. Lidija Jung. You're Korean, right? So am I."

"I am, but no, I just did it, and had it shaved. It used to be long, black. Like you. But I have to get it long, for ballet. I found Jin Han's photos, online, while you'd gone inside. I love what you do. Jin, will you help me with an updated headshot?"

"I wish I could," I said. "It isn't quite what I do, though."

"So, you—"

"Lidija, don't move."

I lifted the camera again. Photos burned up all striving. It was a harsh, ill-paid calling, one I failed with each image I shot. Nothing satisfied; I aspired to a height, the eidolon image, I might die not having gained. But still, if it's going well, I turn powerful. I have my hair pulled high, topknot rising to God. I stop time. I've stolen fire, and I paint with light.

·

She'd folded, slim torso lying flat.

"Tell me what it is you do," she said, sitting.

"With how it's going, I should call it what I can't do." I issued a laugh, as if at a joke. Lidija didn't smile. It wasn't a joke; I'd forced the laugh.

"In that case, what do you want?" Lidija asked.

I exhaled, thinking. I had this idyll, a long, charmed night. Lidija's life had but slight overlap with mine; facing less of the usual comet's tail of sequel, I might risk being honest. I said I hoped to take pictures able to go on living after I died. Shows touring the globe. Prizes; apical honors. Photos up on curated walls, to join the images that first called my name. Notable catalogs. Scholars' articles; top plaudits. I didn't covet fame, though. I knew it to be pyrite dross, a tinsel jinx. Image had nothing to do with public laurels. Photos, art, eluded the lexicon of capital. But I'd shore up life for the pictures while I still could. I'd fight to help the art persist.

I paused. I hadn't, though, said this often. In public, I hid. I'd stop talking, I said, but Lidija replied, "No, Jin, I want all this. Ballet's short-lived. It can't last past the instant it's performed. Not in its true shape." In film, much of a ballet's spirit was lost. One had to learn in person. Ballet passed through bodies, its steps etched in flesh. With each ballerina's dying, a library fell to ruins.

•

Irving set the firepit alight. Most people had stayed inside. I filled Lidija in on Philip, the enduring dispute. I didn't tell people about it, I said; I shied at being pitied. But I was high; Lidija listened. I'd known, as long as I recalled having an I, that I didn't want a child. Still, I was told I had to be wrong. Until I was a parent, I didn't love yet. It was the point of a life, what I was put on earth to do. Paired with the right man, I'd wish to give birth. It was selfish, not desiring a child. I'd learn. God's will. I'd abjure this past, addled self; ill with aching, I'd find I'd long to fill a parent's role. But I didn't; Philip had.

"What will you do?" Lidija said.

I hadn't figured it out, I began saying, but a sharp, tall shade divided firelight.

"Mind if I join you?" he asked, his hand on my chair's top slat. "I'm Ralph."

I said, "No, we're talking."

"Just sharing this fire," he said, moving to sit.

"It's a private talk."

"I'm not going to bother you ladies."

"No," I said, turning. The fire shifted; a log fell, spitting light. I heard Ralph's stride retiring.

Lidija had lain back, legs to the side. But as he left, she sat upright, posture rigid. "Jin, who's Ralph?"

I outlined Quin's words. "She said I could tell you. Quin's Asian. No one else is, just us, so—"

"Oh."

"Quin didn't tell me what Ralph did, though."

"It's enough."

"Let's not spend more time on him."

"You're right," Lidija said. "I'll forget Ralph, but thank you for telling me."

She reclined again, falling quiet. It wasn't the truth, not quite, that I hadn't figured out what I'd do, with Philip. But it was slight, a wisp, the little I had of a plan. It might drift upon the next strong wind.

In short, Philip, I thought I'd wait. I'd avoid telling him I felt jilted. Forlorn. Philip said that, if he could, he'd stifle the urge. So, I'd bring him back, like a hexed dupe of myth, to the lost, true Philip. One not able to pick this made-up being, a fiction, above his living wife.

.

But also, I'd asked Philip what he might lack. It's the old snake-hipped logic, this alluring song. If I'm the person at fault, I can still put it right. Not long before Philip said he did want a child, I'd asked what else he'd like trying, in bed.

"Nothing," he said. But I pushed. Insisted, until Philip said, "Jin, I think I'll ask this of you."

I said no; it was Philip's turn to push. I'd brought it up. He'd be open. I had to be lying. He didn't let it go. Like so, we'd begun dating. Philip had started as a friend. Long enough that, by the time he invited me to a night, with him, at a bistro I loved, I'd thought it fine to bring a third person, a friend. Philip tried again with, he figured, legible dates. Pop-up sushi. Sailing on the Hudson. Estate-sale touring. Still, I brought friends. He pulled me aside, one night, to explain. Startled, I declined. I didn't intend to risk losing Philip. In college, friends lasted. Couples didn't. "Dating isn't an ending," Philip had said. One date, he argued, until I'd given in.

I ought to tell him, I thought. But the night I woke Philip, I halted. In hiding, I was safe. Buried, perhaps, but still living. I cried; folding me in his arms, Philip asked that I let him in.

"Philip, you won't like this," I said. "But I—Philip, I wish you'd hurt me."

.

She put logs on the fire. It hissed, sparks flitting. I asked Lidija to tell me about her life.

"Sure, but what?"

"I'm talking more than you. Tell me what you don't confide to a lot of people."

Lidija, she said, had lived in New York for ballet, during high school, for a few months. Paying for ballet, Lidija's mother had a third job. Ill for a while, she'd kept it from Lidija. She died; Lidija didn't find out until the ballet program ended.

"But the part I can't face is that she was right. If I'd left New York, I might as well have quit. Instead, I got invited to join. It was a last gift, not telling me. Jin, I didn't have to pick. In the end, I don't regret, at all, what she did."

.

Poised on the tip of a board, a tall, naked woman dived. She left a slight ripple, a ghost's breath, before gliding to the wall. "Now you, Jin," Lidija said. "I just told you what I kept silent. You go."

I had to glance past Lidija's head, rifling for ideas. Floret-tipped vines, binding the wall; a garden pergola. Pallid, staring busts, lofted on plinths. Ripe loquats glinting. It was plain Lidija would be insulted if I tried saying anything kind. Pride holds a person up. But in eleven years with Philip, I hadn't left much unsaid. Noticing the busts again, eldritch, figured like souls held captive in marble, I thought of the gallant being who'd dived as if flying, then of the kisaeng's ghost.

I told Lidija the tale as I'd heard it: illicit love, the pine. Reprisals, the talk of a lasting spirit. Hans who, as if misled by a hostile ghost, had upended lives, and died, for love. I thought often of the kisaeng, I said. I didn't get a lot of Han stories, the past kept in hiding. Instead, I had just shards, flashes of rupture, pain. Of longing, from which I'd shaped a fragile bricolage, its edges sharp, with rifts so large I'd clung, perhaps, to the little I did get, all part of this reputed hex. If the kisaeng had wed as she hoped, she'd also be, to my knowing, the first Han artist. I didn't believe in this curse, though, I said. If nothing else, on principle. I'd given up, at a high price, one pile of magical beliefs. I refused to live afraid of a spirit.

I felt light with daring, floating high. Still, I did ask that Lidija not tell a single person what I'd said. I recall Lidija's face as I spoke: intent, rapt, as she'd listen all night.

"But you didn't tell Philip about this?"

"Not yet."

"If you're telling people in your family, then—"

"No, I will," I said.

"Why haven't you?"

"It's about a ghost. He'd think it's nothing."

"Isn't that what you think?"

"Yes, but—"

Lidija waited. I didn't go on; she added a log. Fire leapt, fresh sparks bright, the old tale fading. Did ghosts' spite last this long? Or so I began asking, that first night in Marin.

•

Philip had jerked back after I told him what I'd want. He fell quiet. In a panic, I pled with him to talk.

"Jin, it's, hold on. If I'm going to be honest, it's a lot. I'm not a brute."

"I'm asking you to be a brute?"

"I don't hit people. Jin, I'm not violent. It's a first principle. Boys don't hit a girl."

"It isn't violent, though. Not with consent. I—"

"I just, let me think. Jin, I'll get used to this."

•

"Caged birds," I said. Or so people had called kisaengs, who—

Lidija angled forward, alert. She'd once lived with a man

who'd applied this epithet to Lidija. His kept bird, he'd said. Lidija, his caged starling. But he'd had to let Lidija go.

Lidija was still talking, but a shout rang high. It was Ralph, who'd had a fall. His legs curled, fetal. Red spilled on pale slate. Ralph yelled, flailing. He bit, hissed, wild with pain.

"I'll call for help," Philip said. He'd rushed out, as had all of Irving's guests, the group flocking to Ralph.

Irving argued with him. Ralph didn't need a hospital, he said.

"It's his head," Philip said. "I'll hide the drugs. Medical training, any of you? No, well, first-aid training." One of Irving's friends lifting his hand, Philip asked that he coax Ralph to let him help.

Philip strode in. "I'll be right back," I told Lidija, and followed him. Relating the facts of Ralph's fall to his phone, he picked up bottles littering the house. He put Irving's pill stash in a hall closet. I hid the trash bag full of plastic in a bathtub. In a swirl of carnival lights, people swept in, then left, taking Ralph. He'd be fine, one said. Not to fret. The hospital would get him stitched up. Partiers dispersed, chatting fast, still high.

Philip asked if we could talk, but I'd told Lidija I'd return. "Join us," I said.

"I'll find you, in a bit," he replied. "Jin, we should talk ab—"

"But not tonight."

"I didn't will this to happen," Philip said, dejected.

"It'll be all right," I said, touching Philip's head. I had faith in what I told Philip, that we'd be fine. I left Philip with a light kiss, his lips soft; Lidija was still at the firepit.

"He's capable," she said. "Philip. Not bad in a crisis."

"Once, to explain his job, Philip said, 'I fix shit.' It's film producing, but that's his forte. Solving issues. Putting out fires. If the world's ending, people will ask for Philip's help. I'm glad Ralph's gone, though. Even high, I'm just relieved. Is that terrible?"

Lidija said, "I wish I'd pushed him."

I laughed, surprised.

"What, don't you?" she said.

"No, you're right. I do, too."

She glanced about, bright head flaring. Others had all gone in. Ralph had left a puddle. Prints led through it, a spectral traffic. Lidija bent at the hips, folding in half, lithe, to press her hands to the liquid. She turned up her palms, the floral red unfurling, Lidija's hands like spring poppies. With my phone, I shot Lidija. Stained hands open, full of petals. I have that picture still.

2.

No, I won't tell you what I'm fucking named. Oh, you thought, If I'm polite. Stuck-up, trifling Han bitch. But first of all, let's get this straight. Pah, I'm howling. I'll be dipped in shit. So, you jerks still think I died to be with him?

3.

Irving offered us all a second pill. I relaxed, prodigal again. Nothing had to end. Lidija and I kept talking. Partiers sped, nude, to the pool. Blue nereids, plume-tailed. Lidija clapped; divers laughed, telling us to get in. "Not yet," Lidija called.

I said Irving had talked about Lidija being a stage name. She flushed along the high slope of her face.

"Lidija," she said. "It's a white girl's name. Ballet's full of white people. I regret it, though, being prudent. I wish I'd kept the name I had at birth."

"Which is?"

"Iseul," she said. 이슬. "I love that you're called Jin. If I could, I'd be Iseul again."

Philip also had a birth name, Felipe. Once the Seligs lived in New York, not San Isidro, his parents had figured infant Felipe might as well be Philip Selig. His skin ran pale. Philip had tried to be Felipe again; his parents fought him. I should go to him, I thought, but Lidija tousled her head, the radiant pelt. I'd heard of it being a harsh shade, the white; it left follicles stripped, fragile. Lidija's life relied, for the most part, on white people's ratings of bodies on the stage. Often, hers might be judged foreign. But she didn't want consoling.

Instead, I said that, in the last rush of toiling on triptychs I'd exhibit, I slept so little, I'd take naps on the studio ground. "It's just a studio in Philip's and my place, down the hall. But often, late at night, I'd get so tired I'd fail at taking those last steps to bed. On trips to New York, I'd sit in the gallery's space for hours. I studied the light. I'd log charts, plot graphs. Back home, I built its space, desk-sized. I'd tack little photos to doll walls. No detail felt trivial. I kept being a pain. But also, I didn't turn down a single request. I told Chi, the gallerist, that, if it'd help, I'd pose naked in Times Square."

"Did you?" Lidija asked.

"Pose naked in—god, no."

"But you would?"

"It's just my body," I said.

Lidija let out a loud, abrupt laugh. People's heads flicked. She didn't mind; Lidija, I thought, isn't going to admit a false laugh past her lips. It was evident in the laugh's full pitch, its built-up mirth.

"I'd love, if you're willing, to talk about dancing," I said.

"It's ballet, not dancing, first of all."

"So, right, I'll stop talking," I said, but she laughed again.

"I'm joking." Other dancers poked fun at ballet's elitism. Call it risible, but to Lidija, it was a life. She might be fit for nothing else. It felt as though Lidija's true self lived not in a person, but in ballet. Lidija didn't feel alive, not dancing. Not half-alive. "But up to a minute ago, I was using crutches," she said. "So, I spend a lot of time with a physical therapist. I go through drills in a pool, holding the tile edge. But I won't be at full strength until, earliest, this fall."

"Is it hell, not dancing?"

Lidija hesitated.

"No, forget the shit I just said."

"Jin, it's fine. It's what they'd all figure, that I'm in hell. No one's said it, though. I don't mind, at all, the physical trial. But if I'm not dancing ballet, I'm, well, in a lot of pain."

Halting, afraid of a second misstep, I said, "It's not the same thing, but, since last June, I can't take a picture I find worth saving. In high school, I said I'd pledge my life to God. I was a disciple of Christ. But I left the faith, along with, for a while, the will to go on living. I don't tell a lot of people this, but I think the photos kept me from dying. If I lost that, I can't figure out what I'll do."

"So, I'll help," Lidija said, blond head tipping back. "I'll inspire the next spell, an epoch, of Jin Han's photos. People will ask how it began. One night, you met Lidija Jung. Images of this Jung, a ballet icon, ended up being the first shots you kept."

I laughed, wishing I had the right words to persist with asking Lidija about ballet. In time, though, I'd be fluent. I'd learn ballet argot, turning expert in the jargon of pliés, tendus, ballon, fifth position; the corps, a principal. I'd fill notepads with lingo, inking line drawings. Spotlit, Lidija lifts a muscled leg with each spin. She flings drops of light, sparking a black, chalked stage. Inhaling lamp-burnt dust, I watch. I photograph. If I could, or so I thought, I'd lap up the drops. Leg high, she whirls again. Pale skirt rising, she floats stage left.

·

I had to find Philip, I said. She'd get a drink, Lidija replied. No sign of Philip in the garden. Not in the kitchen, living room, but I'd find him. I paced through Irving's friend's house, spilling light as I went along.

If I couldn't take pictures, I did still have the light. I'd held, until I didn't, that His will gilded all of living. Rayed light falling, I'd sight the long fingers of God. Since then, I'd had to begin noticing that which exists for its own, fugitive being. I'd attend to details, flitting past. No photo will repeat; prism-split, the light won't hold. It glints, then opens, flashing. Shive-light drifts through.

I found Philip at last, dozing by the hearth. He'd lodged his legs behind a tall urn. I trailed a fingertip along slight lines at Philip's eyes, his full-lipped mouth. His chin, tilting. I laid a hand on his lush, exposed stomach. I sat with Philip awhile, hoping he'd wake up. He hadn't slept well, though. Nor had I. Out in the hall, I ran into Lidija.

"Oh, there you are," she said, with a sigh. I slid down the wall. She followed. "Did you talk to Philip?"

I told Lidija how I'd found him. He was tired; before Irving's, we'd had the usual fight. Philip said he kept thinking of the child we'd have, a little girl. But I'd also pictured this ghost child. I'd tried, for nothing, to wish as he did. Half-pint wraith, she'd be bold, wild-haired. Bijou daredevil, she'd leap from heights. Top of her class. She'd be willful, this avid girl, but leveled with Philip's calm. His loyal spirit. Philip would hoist the girl up to a ceiling. Up, she'd yell. Up high. Small legs kicking, this risk-loving child. Up again.

•

I asked Lidija how she'd known ballet would be her life.

"One night, I went to the ballet," she said. Upflung arms held dancers high; after a girl lifted her leg, it fell slowly, fluttering, like a wing folding. Lidija's child legs dangled. Iseul's, then, but she, too, had wings, hiding in sharp blades lining her back. No one had told Lidija such wings existed. "Ballet's image is a myth. People think it's about being fragile. It's a lie we depict, playing nymphs, sprites. But Jin, I fell in love with its strength. I had to take flight."

Curtains falling, Lidija declared she'd also go on stage. Head rising, arms high, she dipped in place, silent, dancing. Lidija would learn, in time, that her mother had pined for a life in ballet. But as a girl, in Korea, she'd lacked the option. Elders, appalled, had put an end to dancing lessons. Scandal, they'd said. No decent girl danced in public.

"You want to dance on stage?" her mother asked.

"Yes," Lidija said.

"It takes years to be a ballerina. It's hard. Is this what you want?"

But Lidija's head was shaking. Impatient, she replied, "I am a ballerina."

·

Lidija and I went back to the patio chairs. I heard a splash, then hollering. One of Irving's friends had slung him in the pool. Irving kicked to its edge, clinging. Insulting his friend. Both laughed.

On the night I told him, Philip asked why I'd want as I did. I flared up, brave, for once, saying it didn't merit asking. "It's part of who I am," I'd said. I thought to add, but didn't, that it's not just a futile question. It can be malign, hitched as it is to bad, old ideas pairing desire with illness. To put forth an origin is also to begin finding a cure. Philip, as I cried, had pulled back his first replies.

"Jin, I'm trying," he said. He held me, his grip tight.

Philip, here's what I'd explain, if I could: for so long, I'd lived thinking I ought not exist. Not, that is, with an ideal life worth having. In films, books, I was, at best, a punch-line figure. Paper-doll misfit. If not a joke, a villain. Once, a photo legend had given a talk in Florida; health failing, she didn't like visiting the U.S. She lived in Capri. I had to plan a long-haul trip, driving hours, to attend. Pilgrim again, I'd gone. "It's all licit, in photos," she said, during this talk. "Nothing's judged filth. Including sexual kinks, alas."

Circled in light, she laughed. Much of the hall joined in. I laughed along.

•

Still worse, this desire aligned with ruling ideas of what an Asian woman will be: pliant, subject. Ill-used, and glad of it. Just born to serve, the local girls, I'd heard a white man explain, in a Seoul tea shop. It, this lie, brought us terrible pain. Upon, in part, its basis, we kept being abused, vilified, hit, raped, and killed. It was the abiding, evil notion I tried, with how I spoke, moved, and dressed, to fight, a public self shaped to resist this false image I despised. Starting last June, I'd resolved that, as long as I held a spotlight, I had to avoid failing us. Here I was, though, still a betrayal.

·

"Jin, I noticed you as I arrived," Lidija said. "Big hat, not taking a dip. Sitting with Philip's head in a skirt-draped lap. I had to find out what he might be saying. Jin, the focus. If the world fell apart, right then, you'd have kept staring at him."

"Philip hoped to talk, here, tonight. It'd help, he thought, being high."

"Will it help?"

"It's possible," I said. "But he fell asleep."

"Should you get him up?"

"He's had a tiring month."

"It sounds as if you had a hard month, too, though."

I didn't say anything.

"Oh, no," Lidija said. "I have a napkin. Jin, take it. I'll shut up."

·

Still high, I had the urge to dance. Lidija had trouble picking a song to suit me. I can't be polite tonight, I thought. Not by lying.

"Try this," she said.

"It's not right."

"How's this?"

"Not at all," I said.

"Okay, what about—"

"No, it's still too—"

"Fast?"

"So, listen," I said. "It's inviting. By lilting, right here, this song is asking, Will you dance with me? Its bass line is, ah, how to put it, mild. If I tried dancing, I'd have to think with each step. But I'd like a song willing to tell me what to do."

She picked a song. I objected, but Lidija said, "Hold on." I waited; the song rang in a third line, adding depth, swing, a firm, driving thud. I jumped up, dancing.

*

Lidija and I sat in the hall. She was quiet; so was I.

In that lull, a thought stirred. I might be able to confide in Lidija about what I'd told Philip I wished he'd do. It formed, this inkling, a dim, floating shape. Hours ago, I'd asked if Lidija was close to Irving. No, she'd run into him in the Haight. Irving had to remind Lidija of how they'd met. Our lives didn't overlap. She, unlike Philip, had no existing high opinion of me that I might lose. Maybe, if I'd recite it again, I'd find less baffling words for Philip.

I told Lidija what I'd said to him. For a decade, I'd tried

telling Philip. But, until a month ago, to no avail. Philip had, though, given it a shot. I'd bought props. He'd hit me a couple of times. Philip then said he'd take a break. He was upset; I, then, repelled him. I laughed, in part to hide what I felt, how soiled, wrong, I'd known I had to be, craving the filth I did. "It's a little abrupt, Jin," he said. Foiled, we'd ordered late-night pierogi, then gone to bed. I'd lain awake, thinking. I'd get him a how-to guide, I'd told Philip. But I did have one. I'd read it; I'd folded pages, scoring lines. I hadn't given it to him. Not yet. Should Philip recoil from that, as well, I had no idea what I'd do.

I had my legs drawn up, head in rigid arms, as Lidija said she knew people who might be helpful. Dancers didn't get paid well. Sex work, for those not born rich, tended to be an option. Lidija had a ballet friend who'd also, on the side, hit people for cash. She'd left ballet, but still hosted small parties, here, close to Union Square. In fact, this friend, Hilde, was hosting one next Saturday night. It was just for women. If I'd like, I might go, with Lidija. It wasn't filth. Nor odd. It moved Lidija, how artful bodies will be, retelling old stories. She didn't—

"I have to stop talking about this," I said.

But if—

"No," I said. "Lidija, I can't."

She stopped.

•

Philip had sculpted, in college, with salvaged objects. It was, for Philip, just sport, he'd said. Not like the temple I'd built of image. But I loved his deft, pell-mell work, alive to trash. He'd sight glories in a busted pipe; I'd gone with Philip on his field trips to thrift shops, the junkyard. I helped him pick through the shoal at low tide, chasing flotsam. Philip scraped the mold. He wiped bird shit, scaling littoral rot. So, if Philip was going to be repulsed, even Philip, well.

•

It was late, the high dissolving. Most of Irving's guests had left. I had a rule that I'd quit at one pill, two if I felt like reveling. But Irving still had more.

"I want a third pill," Lidija said.

One of Irving's friends protested. She'd regret it in the morning, he said.

"I don't care," she said.

"You're sure it's what you want?" I asked.

Lidija closed her eyes, reflecting. Thin lids glinted with faint gold. In the ceiling lamp's glare, dust spun, whirling as it fell. "I'll take half a pill, if I'm not alone."

"I'll do it," I replied. Others then said they would.

I halved a pill for me and Lidija. She said she'd get in the pool. "Jin, I think you should find Philip," she added, disrobing. Lidija walked outside, lace-fretted bra straps binding folded wings. Philip, in the living room, still dozed, head poised on the hearth. I lifted Philip's head, tucking a leg to his nape.

Philip's face was brick-stippled, flushing. He slept like a child, tight fists balled at his chin. You didn't find me, I thought, but no, I had to be just. It wasn't Philip's fault; we'd bridge this rift. Let him rest tonight.

So close to the fire, Philip had gone florid, hot, as if he'd ignite, but I'd watch. I kept vigil; after a while, the last pill fading, I called to him. I didn't want Philip to wake up cold, head aching. He balked, tired, until I said he'd have to take, at most, five steps. I helped him to the couch, pulling a blanket over us. Philip flung a leg over mine, then slept. I thought I kept him safe from pain.

4.

Oh, I had a life that began well. I did just as I liked. Ordered not to climb a wall, I'd scale it, quick. I crowed along with the birds. But when I was six, a blight rotted the village harvest. It was cold. People died. I got thin. My parents, hapless, sold me to a kisaeng house. I'd eat well, my mother said, dressing me for the trip. She loved me; we had to part. Don't forget this.

Stop crying, I said. Pah! I let nothing slip if I put my mind to it.

It was the last time we spoke. But I was right. I didn't forget.

5.

Philip and I walked to the airport gate for St. Paul. In the car, driving from Marin, he'd asked to talk about the fight. Not before St. Paul, I'd replied. Sahaj Jain, the friend getting wed in St. Paul, lived a short walk from us. Philip and I saw him often, along with his fiancé, Julian Noh. I'd loved Sahaj, a poet, since college; I shied at being upset, tonight. I'd be joyful for Sahaj.

But the plane, rolling, jerked to a halt. I thought of what I'd told Lidija, the oath I'd defied. "Bit of a lag, folks," the pilot said. More waiting; the plane lifted.

I pulled up, again, the note from Nigel Hugh. He'd asked that I provide details on what I'd give them. Nigel, curating the group show I'd said I'd join. It didn't have to be long, he said. Just a few lines; plus, if I could, a line on the show's title. It had to do with evolving. I was late replying. Still, regret piped, shrill; I closed Nigel's note. I'd told Lidija what I'd pledged I'd hide, last night.

I picked through jots, hints, the slim bits I'd heard of a kisaeng's lot. She, this alleged spirit, had lived before the colonial epoch. Most girls, back then, being kept illiterate, stifled, men loved a kisaeng's erudite mind. She played music with high skill; painted. Flirted, joked, and sang. Noted sijos, kisaengs' poems, had survived. But a kisaeng retired young. If she lacked a rich patron, she might die. In this harsh milieu, one kisaeng did find love. It was short-lived. I'd be hostile, too. But I'd invited this spirit's reprisal. Fretful, I asked Philip what he was doing.

"Reading a script," he said.

"Will you tell me about it?"

"It's set in a palace," he said. Lisbon, the past. Rival fado singers. Hilltop citadel, falling ruins. Foul plots, an evil prince. Six drops of the witch's potion. Royal birds in flight, tails bristling; I slept.

·

Philip sped us to the hotel. I laced up a floor-length dress; Philip knotted his tie. I had a silk noil wrap. I posed for Philip, with a flourish. Philip whistled, as I'd known he might. I laughed, and we left the hotel. It was a swift walk to Sahaj's wedding. Philip and I got in place with time to spare.

Hitched, Julian and Sahaj ran down the aisle, a linked fist raised high. Out in the garden, we spoke to old college friends. I'd quit all social media, last June, desiring quiet. Philip didn't use it; we had large holes in gossip. People filled us in. Sitting at the allotted table, I had Philip to the left, and a friend of Sahaj, Nalini Jothi, to the right. I hadn't talked with Nalini in a couple of years, since Philip and I lived in New York. Until the spring, Sahaj had lived there as well.

"I still miss Sahaj," Nalini said. "Julian, too. I can't believe they left."

I asked how she'd spent time with them.

"Oh, the usual. Bars. Dinners. Sahaj and I went thrifting. Opera. Jin, Prija, my wife, tried to buy a triptych. But they'd sold out. Next time, she'll jump on it. Hi, Prija, I'm talking about you."

Prija raised a glass. With thanks, I asked Nalini, "Did you also go to the ballet?"

"Often, with Julian," Nalini said. "But Prija won't, so she'd drink with Sahaj. Julian and I tippled, as well, during the ballet. We'd all go out dancing. But Jin, are you a ballet fan? If so, let's get you and Philip back to New York. I insist."

I exhaled, afraid. Nalini's face dipped, eyes large. I felt cut open, laid bare. But I had nothing to hide. "I wish I did go to the ballet. Last night, though, I met Lidija Jung. She—"

"Lidija *Jung*?"

"Lidija Jung, right." Lidija's name, echoed, rang like a conjuring. She might take shape, here, in St. Paul, triple-called.

Nalini put down her glass. "Did Lidija talk about why she left?"

"No, what?"

"It might not be true, but I'm told she's left her position. If it's true, it'd be a wild upset. If a dancer's rising, hers isn't a place one quits. Lidija's young, the first Asian principal. It has to be tiring. But did you watch Lidija's dancing?"

"No."

"Oh, you should. Lidija's grand jeté, its ballon, Christ. It's such thrilling ballet. One sold-out night, I sat up high, in the back. Even so, I wept at Lidija's fingers. Lidija's toes! I'm going on too long. But if Lidija Jung quit, it's odd."

"She's injured," I said.

"It's not what I'm told," Nalini said. "People are saying she's all right, but that she left. Ballet's a small village. If Lidija did quit, we'll find out."

I got the phone from my bag, with a plan. I'd stop talking to Nalini. If Lidija had lied, fine; if not, how painful, to face doubt about being, of all things, injured.

Lidija had asked for a headshot, again, before Philip and I left Marin. "I'll be in town until the fall," she'd said. "Irving will put us in touch. Don't say no, Jin. Let me hope." I hadn't said yes. But I'd also kept the light-addled photos I'd taken of

Lidija; useless, as prevised, they'd still lived past a single image I'd shot in months. I'd told Lidija so much. If it might help with pictures, though.

I'd asked Nalini about ballet with a slight, risible hope. In the spirit of giving it a whirl, just taking a shot. But Nalini had met the hope; she'd hailed Lidija's name. It was a failing, this abiding lust for signs. I held the phone. I flipped it in my palm, idling. I'd had a plan, but what did I—

Oh, I thought. No. I slid the phone in its bag. I'd had the urge to elicit 엄마's gloss of Lidija. She had a gift for divining people's qualities with a photo. "Not based on a person's face," she'd said. "It's the spirit, shining through." I used to laugh at the claim; still, with each photo I sent, she didn't get it wrong. "His heart is open, trusting," she'd said, of Philip, as I began dating him. "His life spills with love." I'd called Philip a friend. It was a partial fib, one she didn't forget.

I didn't send Lidija's picture. I'd had a note, this spring, from a gallerist living in Seoul. "I'm an old friend of your parents," she'd said. She rejoiced they'd moved back, at last. Such glad hours she'd had, long ago, in the Insadong house. I'd still lisped, then; I toddled, but Jin Han's art papered the walls. She'd love to talk again, the next time I paid a visit to Seoul.

So, I had parents living in Seoul. Not, as I'd thought, in the U.S.

•

엄마 had pled for Church nuptials, with a priest. Or she'd skip the wedding. 아버지, as well. But I'd be obliged to go to Noxhurst five, six times, with Philip, to solicit the local priest's aid. I'd ask a rigid celibate to provide help, advice, on conjugal living. Philip had no religion. I'd abjured mine. Even while I did worship, I'd relied on a less papal gospel. Fine, I had quit the faith, 엄마 said; trifling, she thought, a child's false step. Prodigal, hailed with angels, I'd repent. But failing to have Christ preside at nuptial rites: that, the Church judged a cardinal sin. It left us both, Philip, me, in mortal peril.

"엄마, I can't begin this part of life with lying," I'd said.

I asked Elise, a friend, to preside. Philip's kin, the Seligs, piled into Noxhurst. 엄마 kept her word. It had to end, this fight, I figured. No, she'd go silent, 엄마 said. Until I'd give in. Pious, licit nuptials, with a priest. I still, per the Church, lived in sin. "It's not just you, darling." I'd birth a pagan child: I'd spoil this made-up infant's soul. In the past, 엄마 and I talked often, confiding. But again, she kept her word. So did I, though.

•

I lift the burnt scraps of what's left, going through rubble. It's plain this fight led to not telling Philip about the kisaeng. I had, in fact, split my family apart. If the ghost's curse did find me, 엄마 had said, I'd have the urge to ignite existing ties for a futile, single love. I'd then burn down my life. But loving Philip, it wasn't futile. Nothing had gone up in flames. I didn't intend to give Philip the idea that, by siding with him, I thought I might be playing out a spirit-inflicted hex. I valued Philip's logical mind. His mother, raised Catholic as a girl, had broken with the Church. For, she said, colluding with the junta's evils. I prized this high-minded rejection of Christ's malign proxies; I loved Philip's infidel upbringing, blithe to all things occult. Deities, expelled. Spirits, kept out. If I did tell him, Philip might laugh; I'd have to join him.

•

On the parquet-tiled square, a gold carpet, the dancing began. People flung down jackets, kicking off shoes, flesh exposed, bare soles loping. I still didn't have a tripod; balked, I shot exulting, silk-hung bodies. Nalini glided past, hands on Prija's hips. I replied to Nigel's note: "I'll tell you when I can," I said.

"Jin," Philip called, from a table. I went to him, thinking of Lidija's jumps. Didn't I wish to learn from this artist who'd push so high? No, I'd leave Lidija alone, I thought, until late that night, after the band stopped, the hotel bar tolled its last call, and we'd left a closing shindig in Nalini's suite. Philip held a plate with a tall, slanting slice of cake.

"I caught sight of a couple, with a kid, dancing," Philip said. "Six years old, jigging as long as you did. One child isn't fated to change people's lives. Not as much, if—"

"Philip, it's late."

"It's after Sahaj's wedding."

"I have to figure out photos for Nigel. I've told you, it's hard, not being able to work. It's, I'm afraid image has left. I'm frantic, Philip. Let's talk after I have Nigel's photos. I have until just this fall."

"Or we can talk about it tonight," Philip said, his voice rising.

"It's not as if rushing it will—"

"Jin, I want this."

I had time, I might have said. I'd be thirty in the spring. But I didn't plan to give Philip false hope. I'd kept watch on the child, too, twirling in his Jodhpuri suit. First, though, I'd noted Philip's face going soft, trailing the child. Philip had talked with the child's parents, asking which songs he liked best. "It's just a few months," I said, instead.

"But Jin, I'm not telling you to—"

"I'm asking you not to yell."

I was shaking. I'd fled the first time Philip yelled while arguing. Noxhurst, late spring; I'd run in the Edwards art building, locking shut a one-person carrel. Even with its high, safe walls, the carrel might quake, panels falling, and I'd be left exposed. Philip slid notes, apologies, across the sill, until I let him in. It had to do with my parents, how they'd fight, I'd said. If a man yelled, I had to run. Philip, in time, had adjusted. But he'd lapsed, this past month, again.

His face pulled tight, sad, Philip said all right. "I won't yell," he said. In the fall, after I'd sent photos to Nigel, we'd talk.

Back in the hotel bed, Philip fell asleep. He'd left his cake slice on its plate. I put it aside, draped with a cloth napkin. On the day after our wedding, Philip and I lazed in bed for hours. He ate the rogel cake his sisters had thought to bring to the hotel. I fed him each bite. Philip rolled on his side, chortling at how full he'd gotten. I asked if I ought to stop. Oh, no, he'd said. I licked milk jam from his lips. The Seligs called, telling us to join the post-wedding brunch. People were waiting. Still, we dallied, being alone as long as possible.

I sat on the bed. Philip sighed, tilting his weight. I tapped the night stand. So often, I'd lunged to rap wood as I thought well of Philip, afraid I'd jinx us with the delight I'd take in him. It was as if I'd jerry-built us a shack, a plain, rough shiel. I'd tried each plank, hoping I'd prove it sound. But I hadn't readied us well enough. I rapped again. In the quiet, trying to be silent, I cried.

Lidija had said Irving could put us in touch; I asked him. Irving replied before I put the phone down. I wrote to Lidija. I'd be glad to talk about a headshot, I said. If I wasn't the right person, I'd help find a local artist who'd suit Lidija. Did she want to get a drink?

6.

I lived in the big kisaeng house. I ate well; as usual, I outdid all the pupils. But this one girl, a kisaeng's child, put on airs. I didn't get sold for coins, she said. No, I replied. Instead, your mother died giving birth. One more inept, whelping bitch. She called me a shit-eating village peasant. Cunt-faced, unloved harlot drip, I said. She ripped my jeogori. I tore up her face. She cried; I laughed. For a long time, the kisaeng's child and I didn't talk again.

7

I walked from the light-rail station to the hotel Lidija had picked.

In the six days I'd had since Sahaj's wedding, I studied. I found clips of Lidija's ballet. Leg bent, she rose high on the tip of a ribbon-tied foot. Lidija spun, fixed upon earth with that one small point. Flaring to life in the brief, official films selling ballet, but I didn't find a single phone-shot clip. Nothing from Lidija's fans. I was left wondering. So little film, with not one parading Lidija's famed leap. She was listed as a principal. Lidija's old portrait: long hair coiled tight.

•

Lidija had said to go to the hotel rooftop. I passed a bellhop, thinking of Elise, the friend who, in college, first said to pursue an artist's life. I had foreign-born jitters. Debt having ravaged my parents, I'd gone to Edwards with help, a full scholarship. I'd object, talking with Elise, to the risk of being indigent. Elise, who'd grown up with less than I did, lacked such qualms. "But you'll regret not having tried," she'd said.

I'd last visited Elise a month ago, after the birth of her second child, Shiloh. I'd taken gifts: top-shelf gin, a lavish robe. Philip had picked up a large plush doll for the first child, Lionel. I thought Elise brilliant, original. She might talk to me about the shots I'd kept of Lidija. Rising past the hotel's ceiling, I sent Elise a line, asking if I could bring hotpot to her place. Bells jangled; in glaring light, I got out.

I told the host I'd wait by the stand. It had a parasol, wide shade. I held open a photo catalog. Images slid along the page, lines wilting. In person, I'd loved this art. Lidija was late; I held the catalog, a stage prop. Still no Lidija.

"Jin, I've kept you waiting. I'll get you a drink."

I turned, jolted by the sight. People shifted, rippled, heads angling to Lidija. Like plants tilting with the sun, I thought. It wasn't just Lidija's face. Lidija's regal bearing, its pride, implied a privilege. One she might stop at will: this right, a bit of wild luck, to glance at Lidija. I did want to take Lidija's picture again.

She paid, adding a liberal tip. I accepted, with thanks, a Collins glass.

"The tables are occupied," Lidija said.

"I can stand, if you don't mind."

"No, it's fine."

"Will your leg be all right?"

"Of course," Lidija said. I pulled out a roll-up hat. She asked what I was doing.

"I burn in direct light," I said. "I'll get hives, a rash. It led to photos, I think. It's the light I'm denied."

"But Jin, you should have said. The city's flush with bars not on rooftops."

"Oh, no. I'm used to sunlight."

"I'd be fine leaving."

"If you're saying you'd like to sit, then—"

"Listen to us," Lidija said. "Such ladies, living to serve the group. I, like you, require not a thing. In fact, I don't quite exist."

Gin spilled as I laughed with Lidija; I put the glass down on a ledge.

"I noticed a bar in the hotel," she said.

"Let's go," I said.

Inside, the place was full. Lidija and I left the hotel. Nothing felt right. Sports bars; a pub, with people caroling, goblets high. On the next block, its slant uphill, Lidija's gait slued zigzag. It helped the injured leg, she said. I thought of what Nalini had implied; I wished, again, that I hadn't asked Nalini about Lidija.

"I live close by," Lidija said. "It's a friend's place. I just picked up a gallon of olives at the—"

"Did you say a gallon?"

"I love olives. But I overdid it. Do you like olives?"

"I do, but—"

"Jin, will you help me with the pile of olives?"

I said yes, I'd go to Lidija's friend's place. It was past the crest of this hill. She hiked left, then right.

"Can I ask what you're thinking?" Lidija said.

"I was going to ask for olive specifics. But no, Lidija, you talk. I talked a lot, at Irving's."

"Oil-cured Beldi," Lidija said. "I let a man, Neil, take me on a trip last fall. I was dating him, then. But during that trip, Neil and I visited a lion refuge."

Upon arriving, long-haired Lidija was told she didn't get to spend time with the lion pride. It wasn't safe; Neil could, though, hair length being the divide. So, Lidija shaved it all. She'd gone with Neil in a cage. The guide bolted its gate shut. Big, intent cats padded to the cage. Intrigued, lions jumped on top. Playful, Lidija said, romping, flat gold eyes shining. The ceiling slats had gaps, to let big cats lick skin. I imagined Lidija's face lifting, the hot, rough tongues lusting at soft flesh.

"I kept shaving it. It gets long fast. Once I'm able to put it up, I'll be on stage."

•

Lidija led me to a high, polished loft. Its light poured in from oblique glass. In a large niche, a barre split the wall. Striped divans ringed a globe, birch logs tidied inside. But the bed's floating, I thought. No, a slim dais, its stage, lifted the frame. Stark, plain walls. Its slate island, kept bare. Lidija slipped off her flats. Neil, the lion cage; this palatial loft. It didn't add up, but I just said, "So, this is a friend's place?"

It was, and he had a London job. He'd be gone until the fall. Oh, the loft had light-filtering glass, for his art. "Jin, you won't burn." He'd put all his art in storage, though. It didn't suit Lidija. "I'll get the olives."

8.

In the garden, I heard singing. I stalked its trilling to the ki-saeng's child, alone. I had to put up with no end of la-di-da caroling, and oh, I played the silk-stringed lute, oh, yes, the flute, piri, harp, and fiddle. Oh, I had gifts, but being a ki-saeng, a captive bird, I'd train to pipe it in the shit-filled ears of rich, dolt pricks. Like playing the harp to a pig.

But this girl's singing, it was all hers. Its lilting pitch tripped up to high notes, halting, a little, at the top. One soft laugh, then she kept going. Simple lines, reveling in the spring, this garden. Not a paean we'd learned. Music just saying, I'm here. I'm living. Out of sight, I stayed quiet. It's not right to startle a wild bird. No, you let it sing.

9

Lidija said she'd fix gin juleps. "I thought, last night, of the juleps you'd left at Irving's. So, I got mint. I lifted a toast to you, Jin."

She turned; I offered help. Lidija declined. But she'd fixed juleps with me in mind; absent, I'd existed to Lidija. She hefted a large mason jar packed with olives. Its lid was tight. Lidija strained to open it, biceps ridging. With the jar base lodged at her hip, she twisted.

"Tada," she said, as the lid spun.

I clapped. Lidija's face altered, the sharp angles sliding open with a laugh. Soft light along harsh lines. Portraits, I used to think, held a glint of His spirit, flashing through. It pulled me to the form. Split, broken vessels: the gaps in people's making let Christ's light spill forth.

Lidija ripped the mint. She didn't often fight with lids. One night, foiled by a lid, Lidija's mother had talked of missing Lidija's father's skill with opening jars. He'd left while Lidija was in junior high, then died. In Idaho, herding cattle. He'd lived with an adult son he'd kept secret. Lidija didn't miss him. Piqued, she'd begun hand drills. She built up her grip until she could open all the jars in the house.

"Here," Lidija said, giving me a highball.

She tapped a glass lip to mine; we spoke of the fires. One had just started in Napa. Lidija spat an olive pit in a napkin, her neck arching. Often, the wind kept smoke from us, I said. Not all of it, though. But if she'd have long hair again, what might Lidija want in an updated photo?

"It's the first time I've had to stop dancing."

I nodded, waiting.

"I want this captured. So that I don't forget."

"Is this for you, or—"

"It's for me."

"It has to be a headshot?"

"Why?"

"If you'd dance, instead," I said.

"Oh, so—"

"Or hold a pose. I might be able to help. But it has to be right to me, first. I can't form the image for hire. I wish I could; it's not that I'm a purist. I tried, last fall, for a fashion gig. It was a flop. Lidija, it's possible not a thing will come of it. None of this might be what you'd want. Should I point you to other people, instead?"

"I'll hold a pose. I just have to avoid putting weight on this ankle."

Lidija raised a leg to the side, then let it drop. She'd injured it while rehearsing. On the stage, during a ballet made for Lidija. It ended with a swift, paired dance, Lidija leaping in a partner's arms. He'd lift Lidija, using one hand, above his head. She'd danced with him, Thijs, the male principal, a long time. Lidija trusted Thijs; she loved him. She had to, with partners, while dancing. People hailed Lidija as a thespian; she didn't act, though. Lidija had to dance as she believed.

On the night Lidija was injured, Thijs had fallen ill. So odd, Lidija thought, his playing truant. One didn't skip ballet for being ill. But Josip, Thijs's friend, also a principal, had studied the role. "It's a big move, the lift," Lidija said. "Still, for Josip, it'd be simple. Instead, as I leapt in his arms, Josip's lift failed. I fell on my ankle. I heard it snap, like a lock turning."

In a ballet article I'd read, a principal, Italian, spoke of the hip she'd injured. She thought, often, the Italian principal said, of a famed violinist who, having injured his hand, praised God he could quit playing music. For the rest of his life, he'd kept his violin in its case, but she plied art through her own form. Each time she'd walk, the Italian principal was thinking of this loss. In her telling, as in Lidija's, I heard a treble ring, the tocsin peal of rage pitched so high that, had I not known the song as well, I'd have missed its call. Piping of exiled worship, love that has mislaid its object.

Lidija put down her drink. "I'll get back to ballet. But first, let's do this, Jin."

"Can you pose while calling up a past, ah, a triumph?"

She lifted a tights-clad leg, tilting it high above her head. Long dress fabric slipped down Lidija's thigh. "How's this? It's the last position I held on stage, before I leapt." Her leg glided up as if pulled by a string. She put both hands out, level with the ground, fingers spread.

"Lidija, wait." I lunged to get my bag.

"Jin, you don't have to rush. I'll hold this."

I tested light, then tried a couple of shots. Sloped, tall glass cast dividing lines, dogleg rails striping Lidija's body like the bars of a cage. Lidija raised her face to lions. It was hot, the wall of glass taking in light, heat. I shot again.

"Let's stop," I said.

Leg floating down, she said, "Did you get what you want?"

"I'll check tonight."

"If you're stopping for my sake, don't."

"But you're injured. I don't want to tire you."

Lidija lifted a leg, posing. "You can't tire me, Jin."

I shot again, slight drops rising from Lidija's face in radiant tiles, fish-scale opals. Lidija, netted, pulled in from pelagic depths. Split-tailed prize, bold skin flaring. In altering light, she blurred. Iris flesh, injured leg tall. She held the pose.

⋅

Once I finished, Lidija said she'd be back. I sat at the island, lap cradling a slant of light. I used to think I'd begun life as a partial fish. In the story of my birth, I'd flung to shore a fortnight late. Birth pangs lasting hours, then days, as 엄마 said she'd kill people if I got forced out before I was willing. She didn't let them operate until told I'd die. I hollered in the doctor's face, as though furious he'd intruded. She loved retelling this hero's epic, taking pride in the strength of will I'd shown, fighting birth. "Oh, no, darling, not by *sea* section," she'd said, laughing. I had no littoral origins. I'd spun to life in her body's soul; I'd tried staying. To split us up, they'd had to rip her apart.

⋅

"Do I get photos?" Lidija said. She'd put on a shirt, pants.

"If they're trash, I'll get rid of them. If not, I'll send you what I can."

Lidija asked what she owed.

"No, but you modeled," I said. "I should be paying you."

"Jin, I asked for the photos in the first place."

"I have no pictures for you."

"But you might."

"Until I do, I refuse to be paid."

She laughed. "If nobody's being paid, I'll get you a fresh drink."

Pushing open a glass panel, she let in a draft. Lidija refilled highballs.

"I read a profile of Jin Han," she said. If I didn't mind Lidija's asking, how'd I begin telling people I felt a pull to all genders? It was still a risk, in ballet, not being straight. It held less peril for men. But for Lidija, it'd bring a cost. She'd tell people, but not yet. I sipped gin; I'd thought I'd be alone, learning about Lidija. Instead, she'd read a profile.

"Philip had known, all along," I said. "Plus, living here, almost no one's straight."

"Still."

"It's not quite as hard, taking up the majority's flag."

I'd added, in the past, that I'd kept in mind the elders who thought it alien, a foreign blight. One striking white people, but not Koreans. I'd help fight the idea that people like us didn't exist, I'd said. For the first time, though, I heard posing. I hadn't lied, but I hid a longing not saluted with big parades, the desire still, often, judged bad, evil, ill, wrong. In articles, I was called brave, daring. I'd let it happen, a fraud given plaudits. Rich praise I didn't begin to merit. Not while I was still hiding, and so afraid.

*

It was getting late, the loft filling with bruised light. Lidija asked if I'd like kimbap rolls; I said yes. Ordering kimbap, she tipped left with a stretch, thin shirt riding up. I noticed a line of script again, ink curling along Lidija's stomach. I asked, at last, what it said.

"Here." She raised the shirt edge, baring a full line of ink. *Et puis vous n'êtes pas l'étoile*, I read. "I had it tatted right after I was injured."

"Is it a ballet saying, or—"

"I'd just started dancing ballet in New York. Inès Paquet, the Paris ballet legend, an étoile, visited. In Paris, étoile is the top level. So few people go that high. I'd watch this legend, hoping to learn. I'd get the kind of balm Inès used: that kind of thing. During breaks, Inès didn't stop dancing. *I'm* taking a break, a corps girl said. Quiet, but snide. I heard the corps girl's jib. Inès also did, though. So, you are not the star, Inès replied. With that, she kept dancing. Inès is still in top roles; after a while, the corps girl quit."

"Do you not like taking breaks?"

"I'm taking one. It's long. I won't again."

Lidija let go of the shirt. I was jarred by what I felt next: a hitch, a quick jolt. Lidija's neck had bent; lamp-gilded, her head flared regal, a living coronet. But she'd exert a pull. It had to be part of Lidija's job, her calling, to cast a dragnet spell. Each night, she'd help bring in a concert hall full of people.

"Jin, how'd you begin taking photos?"

"I loved photos, as a child," I said. Until college, though, I hadn't known it was going to be a life. Once I lost God, light fell on a world He'd left. Each trifling part of which, I'd thought, the Lord had shaped as His gift. His epistles, all up in ash. But during a walk through Edwards with Philip, then just a friend, he'd said he wished the maple hadn't died. I asked which maple. Right there, he pointed, startled. I rushed to the spot. I studied its core, split. Ivied vines circling the hewn, lichen-speckled bole. Sap rot, Philip noted. I'd had a final crisis of faith at this exact maple. I'd lain in dirt, its flailing limbs a refuge, as I pled with God for a sign. Still, I'd failed to notice its dying.

So, that night, I told Lidija, I'd bought a flat of potted vines. I filled a pail with Hudson mud. I caked fluvial silt upon my skin; I strung dangling vines. Back at the maple, I adjusted a tripod. I posed as a nymph who'd spring from the maple's split trunk. I shot a cast-out spirit putting on a fresh, willed form. I'd pitched to the earth as a past Jin, then I'd had to get up, changed.

"I had a place I liked to go, the Point," I said. "It was a ridge, on top of the hill. I'd sit at its edge, in blasting wind. Until photos helped me get back to living, I hoped I'd drift off the ridge."

Lidija nodded, quiet.

"If I didn't have this life in photos, I'd still laugh at the idea that placing art first, allowing it full rule, is selfish." Prints rising with bursts of light, strewn lamps, had lit a path. For a while, I'd lived tangled in pain. Image, photos, let me fight through.

"Why'd you quit the old faith?"

"Oh, the usual logic. It's not unique."

"Such as?"

"Of all the faiths, it can't be the single true gospel. I, it's hard to explain."

She nodded, again. "Do you have plans tonight?"

"No," I said. I'd advised Philip to go drinking with his job friends, film people. He'd be out, hurtling through bars. But perhaps I'd urged Philip to adjust his plans, as I'd asked Lidija to get a drink, with a hope I hadn't quite let in, for when Lidija said her friend Hilde was hosting people at her place, did faint silk push rustling along my skin, or did I make it up, a spiteful ghost jostling past?

"Hilde hosts the Saturday parties I mentioned, with—"

"No, right. Hilde's parties."

"It's at 9:00, tonight," Lidija said. "Do you want to go?"

10.

I didn't make friends with pupils; I hadn't tried. I was the best pupil in the house, heading straight to the top. No point in giving a shit about less gifted people I'd end up losing. Oh, you idle, puling Hans can't imagine the life I had in sight, if I'd lived. But I felt like being friends with the singing girl.

11.

Lidija tipped goji tea from the kettle. "Drink this," she said, filling a cup. "Hilde has a rule of no alcohol at parties. It's to help keep people safe. But we'll just watch, so it's fine. Still, if she picks up on a whiff of gin, she'll tell us to go."

·

It was a short walk to Hilde's place.

"I think I'll go home," I said.

Lidija pushed the front bell. "Is that what you want?"

"Yes," I said. "No."

"Which is it?"

"I can't tell."

"Maybe this will help you figure it out."

•

I sift through ash. In a shred of rubble, here's what I turn up. Philip, the night before, had gone to a fish shop. I'd invited Sahaj and Julian, home again from St. Paul. Philip, refusing help with fish, asked that I mix aperitifs. For a while, at my first bar job, I'd nicked my hands, slicing fruit. I bled on dishrags, lapels, so inept with a knife that I was fired. I'd tried again. People said that, for artists, bar jobs might be ideal. It paid, with fitting hours. In time, I could juice a lemon; I'd slice it, if I had to. But while home, unless Philip was there, I still lived on lox; pili nuts. Dollops of plain olive oil. I ate fruit whole. I ripped its flesh with my teeth, and how, Philip, did you think I'd be willing to raise a child?

In thick gloves, Philip shucked oysters. I'd also invited Nhi Trinh and Helen Ogbazghi, friends living down the block. Helen rang the bell with Nhi, a bottle of tej in hand. I lit tapers, impaled with prickets on thin, fluted stems. Philip ladled stir-fried clams on plates of Job's tears. Sahaj and Helen, to Philip's delight, both asked for his recipe. I brought out the Croft port Philip's sister Isabel had sent.

It was a hot spell, the ash stifling. Napa had its fire. Up north, brush kept igniting. But that night, heat broke. Rain fell; we all, exulting, danced. Once friends left, Philip pulled off my jeans. I held the cabinet edge as he fucked me, his hands gentle. He slept; I rapped the bedpost. Philip had said, at the St. Paul airport, that he'd like time to adjust to what I wanted. He'd go learn about it, on his own. I'd wait, I pledged. I slept like that, clinging to the post. Philip, I didn't plan to risk the life I had with you. I held it tight, I thought.

•

In Hilde's house, Lidija went up a flight. She turned left, pace calm; it wasn't Lidija's first time. Uncoiling a voile wrap, she put it on the bed; I shed a thigh-length calfskin jacket. She handed me a full glass from a small table. I had a sip of club soda, its froth hissing. I followed Lidija to the end of a hall—

But this next part, I see through a veil. In dull light, beige faces glinted. Lidija had said Hilde invited just women; I hadn't known they'd all be white. One person in ripped fishnet tights had wrists pulled high, tied to a ceiling rope. She was being hit with a long-handled whip. Cries rising a pitch, she dodged its lash; the upright figure set the whip down. She knelt by the tied person's side, talking. Both laughed; she picked up the whip again.

People watched; others chatted, quiet. Lidija spoke with a slight blond: Hilde, perhaps. I lifted the glass. I'd finish the soda, then put it down. One person, lace dress bared to its hips, was roped to a post. I felt a sharp pinch on my top lip. It was the glass. I'd bitten through it, taking a shard.

I backed into the hall. Outside, I spat the fugitive shard in trash. I ran; I hit a light, noting the wind. Jacket, I thought. I'd left it at Hilde's; I'd forget it. I loved that calfskin jacket, a thrift-shop find. But I'd lost it, gone. Oh, well.

"Jin."

I halted, waiting. Lidija, striding, toted the jacket.

"I had to go home, and I—"

She offered the jacket. I accepted it.

"I didn't want to bother you," I said.

"Why are you lying?" she asked.

I could just run, I thought. But I still had fresh photos, shots of Lidija. In the triptychs I'd shown, I'd spotlit lustful pilgrims who, for a sight of the desired face, will trek land, beg, hope, abjure, living discalced. I didn't find the pilgrims odd. Not at all. I'd still, if I could, walk His path. For the photos' sake, I'd yield. "I bit the glass I held," I said.

"You what?"

I tapped my lip, showing Lidija a strip of blood. "I bit the glass, so I left."

"Jin," she said. Nails brushed my palm. "It must hurt."

"It's not bad," I said. Pulse slowing, I inhaled. I'd fled; Lidija was still here.

"I have first-aid supplies in the loft," she said.

I slipped on the jacket; Lidija and I started walking. I was quiet. Lidija talked of ballet. In Paris, long ago, a ballet legend had caught fire while dancing. It was a stage hazard. People favored gas lamps' rich light. But the jet fire loved tulle, bending to its fuel. One night, this legend's skirt ignited, melting the outfit top. Dying lasted months, a terrible death.

"So, ballet girl as burnt offering, a shit-paid life used up," Lidija said, the loft bright. "Except, also, the Paris ballet did provide skirts doused in a fire-resisting liquid. By the king's edict, people had to perform in this new, improved cloth. But it wasn't as light. It didn't float like tulle. It hid the dancing. She refused to swap." Lidija brought, from a cabinet, a large box. "I'd have kept the tulle."

She wiped my lip. Lidija's face close, I averted my eyes. It was late; Philip might be home. Gas jets burning, tall flames bowed to each girl whirling past. I'd have kept the tulle, as well.

"Jin, this will hurt, but it'll stop the bleeding," she said, liquid hot on the cut. I held in a flinch; Lidija lifted her hand. "Done." She asked if I'd like a glass of vodka, with ice. "It'll help the lip."

I sat with Lidija at the slate island. Respite drifted past, tranquil, mild. Not long after Philip and I began dating, I'd said that being with him felt as natural as the time I spent alone.

Philip had asked, confused, if I'd pick solitude. No, I'd replied. I was telling him that, for once, I didn't have to pretend.

I slid a toe off the rung. "I'll go home."

"No, wait," Lidija said.

"I should—"

"But you're upset. Jin, please, tell me what's going on."

"I can't believe people have parties for this," I said. "Or, I can, I've heard of parties like Hilde's. But I did go from Christ to Philip. People, at Hilde's, they're all living out what I tried to stop desiring. Not just living. Parading it. I still can't put a name to it. It's hard, finding out it's right here. Did you notice Hilde's guests might all be white? I bit through a glass." I heard the words breaking. "I just left."

Rising, Lidija said, "I'll put on music." In Lidija's first soloist role, she'd had a long adagio, set to a Libich string quartet. She'd played the quartet, at night, so that she'd practice while she slept. Now, though, she hated listening to a piece she'd danced. Not while she was injured. But she hadn't danced to this fast quartet, also by Libich.

I got up to sit with Lidija on a divan. Panic surging, I listed objects along the hearth. Slim candles, the spiral wick still white, set on plinths. Log bin. Tall, glazed urn. Obsidian sphinx, its tail curling. If I'd list items, fixing sight on details, hues, I might quiet the panic. But the Libich quartet's high-pitched strings fell silent, leaving the cellist alone. I began shaking.

Lidija slung an arm upon my back. She held me, not talking, until I'd stilled.

"It was all white people," she said. "I didn't notice, but I'm glad we left."

"Oh, you're being so nice."

Lidija's eyes closed, as if she had to pick out a tune. "Is that not right?"

"What?"

"I'm being nice."

The cellist pushed forward; a violist joined the singing. Lidija said that, at first, living in New York, she'd thought of finding sex work. "I had nothing, a ballet stipend. But then, I dated a man who liked paying for what I lacked, so I was fine. Hilde and I shared a place. Hilde, like me, didn't have rich parents. Instead, she had a side job. One client of hers asked that she bring a friend, to watch. I was paid just to talk with Hilde. It was fetish work. I enjoyed it. He was tied up, and she hit him. I went back a couple of times. Jin, I'm saying I had fun."

"Oh," I said. Ice slips floated on liquid: slim wraiths. One hissed, cracking. I thought of a Han son who, long after the kisaeng's death, had met a girl while ice-skating. Falling in love, they'd eloped. He told his parents what he'd done; his father said, Get out. He'd shied a bottle at his child's head. Dodging, the son escaped. With the north invading Seoul, the Han patriarch fled south, taking his wife and children. His despised son, left behind, expired in a fire, along with his beloved. It was odd, though, for this ill-fated couple to have spoken much in the first place. If not, perhaps, for a spirit's curse. I put down the glass. I fidgeted, hands writhing.

"If I could help you," Lidija said.

I waited, listening for a ghost's rippling silk.

"If I said that, Jin, would I be intruding?"

"But what kind of help?" I asked, quiet. I couldn't tell if she'd heard.

Lidija closed a hand on top of fretful, knotting fingers. "Is it going to be just one kind?"

12.

I got the kisaeng's child to be a friend. Listen, I get what I fucking want. She and I stayed up late at night, hiding. In the garden, I listened to her sing.

13.

Elise and I met for hotpot. She'd refused the takeout I said I'd bring. It was Elise's first time going out since the infant's birth. Shiloh slept, rolled in a lilac sling. I'd spent much of last night helping a shared friend hang his exhibit. Elise asked about the photos. I tried to think of how I'd put it; she noticed.

"No, Jin, don't do that," she said. "Don't be polite."

"His photos are rushed. I could be wrong, but—"

"I doubt you're wrong."

"But he didn't ask, and his show's about to open."

"Oh, right. No."

"If I rush pictures, though, if it's late, you'll still have to tell me."

"I'll tell you."

It was part of why I'd had this impulse to talk with Elise. I'd kept the shots from Lidija's loft. Before I left, I'd told Lidija I'd go to the loft again. I hoped for Elise's advice. She put shallots in hotpot broth. "I'll add the ribeye," I said, stirring liquid.

Elise nodded, chin-length bob full. Invited, last month, to Elise's place, after Shiloh's birth, I'd figured the ruling purpose of a visit was to help. Philip and I might wash, mop, and wipe, I thought, but the place was tidied. Elise's husband, Hiju Pai, offered herb crêpes. It was the life she'd exhibit, a public Elise. Hiju's parents did live close by, in Vallejo. But just before Shiloh's arrival, Elise had spoken, at length, about the photo series she'd finish with images of birth. Since then, Elise hadn't brought up the birth photos.

•

Until she first had a child, I hadn't known Elise to be less than forthright. For Elise's final project, at Edwards, she'd shot people who'd all, during the past month, had an abortion. Images of quotidian life. She'd had objects veiling each subject's face: a bough, a college flag. Just in case, Elise said. In a Noxhurst journal's profile of Paige Idrisi, the artist visiting Edwards that term, Idrisi spoke of rating high Elise's student project. So, the journal published a shot of Elise's work. On talk radio, a host opined that Elise, plus the college, lifted up abortion. Irate locals picketed the art building. One Edwards journal asked Elise if she'd thought of revising the project. Perhaps with people who'd had a child adopted. Or who'd kept the infant. Did she wish she'd picked a less inciting, disputed topic?

"It's not a topic to dispute," Elise said. "It's basic medical help." She, so far, had no fetal pile to abort. But if she did, she'd rip it out, then include the photo. In fact, she'd love this kind of tutelage. She'd just decided, while talking, to find people who'd train Elise in giving abortions. It might be useful, living as she did in this violent, puritan ash-heap of a failing empire. She felt obliged, after all, to the radio host, for having inspired this idea.

Hostile mail spilled in. *Die, bitch; go back to China.* "I'm from Taipei," she said, striking *China*, jotting the right word. "I'll take 'bitch,' though." She'd add this mail to the project. One night, a pipe bomb hurled into Elise's place. It broke glass, but didn't explode. In lieu of telling Edwards, she hung a sign from the sill. It said, in wild, bright red: *I'll find you.* Hate mail, parcels, all fell quiet. It was Elise's triumph.

Right after Edwards, she'd moved to Chicago. I'd kept in close touch with Elise until, after having the first child, Lionel, she'd quit replying to what I said. I sent gifts; I asked to help. Sahaj, other friends, heard nothing; I lived in New York. I had no signal to push through. But then, at last, Elise wrote again. She'd just moved to town. Hiju had a grant funding his own physics lab.

I'd paid a visit, alone, to Elise's place. Open boxes, flaps high, filled the living room; Lionel slept in his swing, milk-dazed, head lolling. Hiju was at his lab. For a while, in Chicago, Elise hadn't talked to friends. She didn't take a photo. Instead, with Lionel's birth, she'd thought of dying. "But I couldn't spoil Lionel's life. He'd find out I'd died of, well, being a parent. So, I went to a hospital. I got help. I lived."

Lionel kicked a leg out from his swing. Elise tensed, but his eyes had shut. She laid a palm on a rising stomach, its shape visible through Elise's white, clinging shirt cloth, and kept talking. She'd tried, with Lionel, to live just as she had before his birth. "I fought the change," Elise said. But with Shiloh, she'd adapt. She'd take photos of her body's altering. Intricate, close-up shots of fold, line, and bulge. Skin that surged with a fresh landscape, a shifting world. She'd log this odd, thrilling trip, natal periplus, of forging a person from flesh. Elise had a stash of old images relating her late mother's life as a girl in Taipei. With the photos overlaid, she'd add expired stamps. Strips of qipao silk. Ink and argil. Gilt; dried tulip petals.

I'd listened, jubilant, trying to be calm. Until days before Shiloh's birth, I then got hotpot with Elise each month. She'd taken shots of fetal limbs writhing, poking Elise's taut flesh. Shiloh's birth, she said, had to give the series its defining form. Birthing Lionel, Elise noted a quaking middle, its half-sphere sliding. Like a globe's plates, making the world. Infant Lionel split a couple of Elise's ribs. She, of all people, had known so little of birth's upheaval.

So, being Elise, she'd dived into birthing annals. It used to be illegal, she'd said, in large parts of the world, talking about birth. Sinful to want help, to long to dull the pain. People got killed for asking. Birth pangs being God's requital, one didn't go against His will. It was still with us, this kind of shit thinking. Elise had a gospel to pass along. She'd use the pain, telling it in image.

Told she'd have a hospital birth, she got the building plan. She graphed light. Plotted tripod angles. She ran drills with Hiju. For the images' sake, she'd refuse all drugs. It was the last I'd heard of Elise's hopes.

•

Broth roiled in the pot. Elise added crushed garlic to dipping oil. I had in mind, I said, Elise's final project at Edwards. Of how she'd replied to bigots' vitriol. "The part when you said you'd rip out—"

"I'd still be able to help, in a pinch." Elise had followed through, as she'd said: finding an activist group, getting trained.

"I love that you can," I said.

Elise, smiling, asked about St. Paul. Hiju's cousin also had a wedding that night. She'd have skipped it for Sahaj's, but this cousin, Jon, had been the first Pai to support Hiju's transition.

He'd argued with elders who thought Hiju ill; Jon sent along articles, in Hangul. Hiju, in turn, called on Pai elders to adjust to his cousin's bride being white. Jon had asked Hiju to be his best man. "Tell me all about Sahaj's wedding," Elise said.

I told jokes, stories; Elise laughed. Sahaj, Elise, and I had met in a photo class, at Edwards. Sahaj, back then, loved image as he did words; for a while, we'd upheld a faith, sharing a temple. Fervid, spilling ale in Noxhurst's late-night bars, we'd talked like high priests, light-stained. Bokeh, we said; metal prints. Depth of field. Focal length. Salt prints. "Do you still have the spot?" I asked. "I do."

Elise pulled back an inch of poplin cloth; she also had it, the slight pit on fragile wrist skin. One ill-judged night, I'd said, to Elise and Sahaj, "Let's pledge to us, this trio, for life." I'd held a key's ridge to a lit candle, then put its hot tip to skin. Sahaj, Elise, also pint-addled, had played along, wailing from pain.

"It's fading," she said. Old scars, though, she'd read, will spring back up. I picked out kelp fronds, the stipes lush, ripe, as Elise spoke of an exhibit she'd viewed, in Chicago. Bird's-eye shots depicting crop lines that popped up in drought-bared fields. Profiles, she said, of henges. Of antique town plans, buried for an Olamic age. Rising like wraiths from soil. But with people, too, flesh didn't forget its past. If we lived to be old, then faded marks like this might rise again. Elise tugged on a fold of Shiloh's sling. "Be right back."

I bathed a radish in garlic-starred oil. But I still hadn't asked about Elise's birth photos. Crop marks; flesh as soil. She might be alluding to birth photos, I thought. I had, in my bag, images of Lidija. Elise sat again. I praised Shiloh's hair, swept high, a profuse shock of black. On Elise's first sight of Shiloh, she'd asked Hiju how, with that head, the child didn't get caught while sliding out.

"Shiloh's birth photos," I said. "How'd it go?"

"Not so well," Elise said. During the birth, Hiju, in charge of the tripod, hadn't spied its falling. Elise didn't blame Hiju. People rushed around, yelling. Elise kept clicking, taking photos. In pain, she didn't give thought to the tripod's well-being; as a result, she had pictures of scrubs, legs. "I gave up on the project," she said, with a shrug. "I have a lot going on, though. It's fine."

•

Elise and I left. She'd walk, she said. It pacified Shiloh.

"I'll go with you," I said. She lived close to the light-rail train I'd take to get home. I didn't add that a serial rapist, still at large, had targeted Asian people in this part of town. She'd spurn the help. I tasted slight ash, the fires in the north burning. But Elise's photos. Months of toil, gone; I didn't push. Isolated, she'd thought of dying. I wasn't failing my friend again.

On a final call with 엄마, I'd said to think of the logic. Such a fight, to defend a fiction. I didn't want to be a parent; nor did Philip. No, she said, I was still being a child. I had no idea what I was refusing. I'd issued to life not just with birth, but in the first Hans. I'd lived along with them, an epoch ago, as they'd abide in me, life going on. "It's a gift, a charge," she'd said. "No one will regret a child."

But often, after hearing I didn't wish to be a parent, mothers had pulled me aside. People confided in me, wild-eyed, choking with regret. One hoped to die while she slept, so that she'd at last gain long-desired quiet, with no guilt. "It's possible, hating being a parent," she said. It should be taught, to kids. Like a health tip. One friend didn't piss alone. Not since giving birth. "It's all I fucking want, but I won't get it," she said. "If I could, I'd go back," a friend's wife said. "I'd pick the life I had, before."

On the path, a child knelt, filling in a paved square with chalk. Elise said, "Is that a dragon?"

With a curt nod, the child said, "I ride her at night."

"Does the dragon have a name?"

"I can't tell you."

"Of course," Elise said. "Is it just for you?"

"Yes, I'm the only girl allowed. I have royal blood, so I ride the dragon."

"Oh," Elise said, taking a step down, to asphalt, a wide puddle. I trailed Elise, thinking, It's a public sidewalk. Irked, I tried to skirt the puddle; an indigo pickup truck, sluing, honked.

"I don't mind if you walk on this," the child said, lifting a small head. I swung, in full, to her side. I'd lie in the puddle. No child so little ought to be this docile. She didn't have to forfeit space. If she didn't fight, they'd take it all. Fill this path with chalk. Ride the dragon, scaled pastel wings open.

Elise said she didn't step on art. The child flushed, and we kept going.

·

I left Elise at her building. I hadn't said a word about Lidija. For a while, confiding, I'd relied on Philip. Only Philip; how prodigal I'd been, how rash. I let him sight past the image I put in the world. One that felt thin, partial, like a garden rated from its skin up, as if foliage didn't rise through rot-fed dirt, topsoil rioting with filth. But with Philip, I'd hacked this image apart. I trod its florid spalls in earth. He'd gloried in this dirt, finding riches, as I did in his.

Philip, for one, hadn't pulled back while I paced the hall, reviling an arts journal for printing a triptych photo with flawed colors. "Give me the heads of the people who did this," I'd said. On a plate, cut fresh. Still dripping. Philip insisted, that night, on taking me out for a lulling drink. He slid his hand in a pocket of the skirt I'd ripped as, quick with wrath, I tugged it on. I didn't notice its split cloth until we'd left the house. Philip asked that I not change. He liked it ripped, he said.

I railed; in Philip's sight, I was diligent. I aspired high. Spiteful, I didn't let an insult go. I had lists of culprits. Devoted, he said, with a laugh. Out of this ignoble dirt, he devised sparkling, lavish gifts. Jay's-nest bijous I saved, lining the hiding spots. So cradled, with twig and soil, I'd built a life with him. One that, to Philip, might not be enough.

I'd said, to Lidija, that I had to explain Hilde's event to Philip. "Is that so?" she'd replied. "It sounds as if you tried to explain. It might be useful to figure things out, first."

The light-rail train arrived. Finding a place to sit, I opened a ballet guide Lidija had advised I read. I'd said, to Philip, that I'd taken pictures of Lidija. She'd model again. It was the first time I'd held this much back from Philip. I hadn't quite lied. But I'd hoped I'd be able to talk with Elise: Lidija, the photos. So, I thought, it's unfit for telling. I can't ask a single friend to help. No one, that is, but Lidija.

14.

THE KISAENG'S STORY, AS TOLD TO JIN HAN

I fell in love. It had to be a secret. She and I, we kept it. Pulled up, her skirt flared open. She had petal skin. Insults attend a kisaeng's life, but she'd also lived in silk, idling in orchid baths. She hadn't pushed grass in her mouth, then dirt, while half a village died. She thought it prudent to trust in, of all the options, people. I shit you not. It left her wide open to this rough, uncaring world. But I'd stand guard.

15

Hours before I'd visit Lidija again, I had a missed call from Chi, the first show's gallerist. Chi didn't call except with photo news; I dialed his office. I'd been placed on a Baptist index of artists to boycott, he said. It had to do with an article stating that I hated Christ. In Chi's mind, the kinds of louts who'd boycott, of all things, photos, should be exiled to art-deprived islands of their own. Go on, be oafs. "I'd forget about it, Jin. It's not a big deal, but I figured I'd tell you. No, it's in print, a Christian journal. If it's what you want, I'll send you the issue."

•

I got asked, at times, if, with the triptychs, I had regrets. "No," I said. But if I could, I'd have put a match to each triptych. I'd take all the photos back. I'd held, for a while, that I felt as if I didn't quite make an image. Ideal, like grace, image might exist before its photo, I'd hoped. I'd find the single living junction of line, hue, and light. If nothing else, this faith let me trust that, when a photo felt right, I'd leap toward it, to yes, I thought. It helped me wait.

For the triptychs, I'd shot religious people in states of worship. Pilgrim sites. Baptist tent revivals. Isolated prophets. I shot while they'd whirl in fits. Dived prone in dirt. Singing, hands lifted, still Christ's disciples. I had the subjects' consent; I'd blown photos large. I paired, with each shot, a self-portrait. I staged photos, acting like the original. Praying, I'd felt as close as I'd get to Him: I also devised short epistles, one-sided calls, to God.

On the day of the opening, I tried getting out of bed; giddied, I fell. Lying on the ground, I laughed. I'd pined for this so long that I'd half-thought I might die first. It was a freight I'd toted until I forgot its heft. But I was here, alive, bale dispelled. Philip asked what the hell I was doing. I tried to explain, chortling until spent. Once I did get up, I rose blithe, exulting. I had the pride of trusting I'd given all I could.

But the first reviews began to publish. Staged jokes, critics said. Brutal, piquant farce. Knife-sharp wit. "It's a hit," Chi said. "I hope you know that, Jin." I'd jibbed, all along, at filling the triptychs with a surfeit of feeling. It kept waking me, at night: did I, by reviving what I grieved, risk indulging in tragic kitsch? Instead, I was called tough, unsparing. Jesting. I was a parodist. I'd pulled off a bold, high-concept joke with images I'd built to be a shrine.

"It's up to you," Chi replied, when I said I'd respond. "But you'd be telling people talking up Jin Han's photos that, alas, they're wrong."

"Chi, that's not what I said."

"Or you'll let all the photos go on living, apart from you."

I'd have argued, still, if Chi weren't right. Bad photos spotlit a slip of nerve, the artist who'd quit. It was the glaring sin of having thought, It's close enough. But with image, there's no such thing; I had, perhaps, held back. I'd played it safe, at the photos' cost. If I'd given up, it was no one's fault but mine I'd failed.

I'd resided, for months, in a flat, blank space. I felt nothing but chagrin. With the idea that I'd beg pardon, I drafted long notes to the people I'd shot. "Jin, I don't think prophets read art critiques," Chi said. So, instead, I mailed each person a small, framed print. I hid the triptychs in a cabinet. I didn't take a photo I kept again, then I met Lidija.

.

She was still thinking, Lidija said, of the kisaeng, plus the Han boy she'd loved. Lidija felt as though haunted by the tale. She didn't find a lot about kisaengs online. Not in English. But like Lidija, they'd danced. Inspired, she'd perused Korean myths, legends, in search of a tale she might adapt into a ballet. "I'm the first Korean ballerina, period, who's had a position in the ranks," she said. "First Asian principal, the list goes on. But I plan to stage a ballet telling our stories. I'd love to fold in pansori. Ribbon-dancing."

I'd paused as Lidija began talking. I zipped a lens in its bag; I'd shot Lidija while she lifted agile limbs. Pointing a flexed leg to the wall, she'd bent a split past the plane line. I set down the bag, asking if she read in Hangul.

"No."

Slight tug of disquiet, sidling past. Did it urge caution? If so, I ignored it. I'd be useful to Lidija. I said I might be able to help find a tale to adapt. In first grade, the principal, a Mr. Biglin, had advised me to be grateful. People like Mr. Biglin had fought to save Korea. I'd asked 엄마, that night, why Mr. Biglin had saved us.

Face rigid, she'd made calls. She pulled me out of the first grade. Until I was born, she'd hoped to be a poet. 엄마 inked, in Hangul, the old tales she'd loved. She etched vivid drawings. In time, she also typed up English classics. Exiling white people's names, she filled living with us. She printed, in linen binding, edges gilded, all the titles she'd adapted. She kept this idyll going until we'd moved to Los Angeles. Once the local shop signs flashed Hangul, she'd put me, at last, in a public junior high.

"But tell me what kind of tale you'd adapt," I said. "Ill-fated lovers, perhaps. Fragile hope, ruin. Is that right?"

"Yes," Lidija said, the laugh belling out. I held in a smile, glad; I'd studied well. Lidija said that, in ballet, people fell in love with a wide span of beings. Sylphs, wilis, spirits, and birds, but a trope did align the bill-topping roles for girls: they'd tend to die of abuse, betrayal. "It's hard, in ballet, to find a male figure worth valuing. I don't want us dying, not in the ballet I'll stage."

"Oh, I love that," I said. I'd sat up, jolted. "People do love a dead girl."

"If we die, we're quiet."

"With no opinions."

"It's the ideal girl."

I asked if Lidija had heard of the crane who'd loved a human.

"Is that the bird disguised as a girl? But no, go ahead."

I spoke; I pictured a table, its black chilgi top. Inlaid pearl cranes lifting from the pond, flying to a lush pine. Scents of figs, loquats, drifting in from the garden. I'd sat in 엄마's lap. She flipped a page, and read.

Once, a crane fell in love with a village man, out fishing. She sighed for him; the gods pitied this bird. Soft flesh hid bristling quills, the sharp bill arching red, forming lips. Spine rising high, straight, in a person's shape, she talked to him. She joined his life as a bride.

But the fish, one spring, ran short. He toiled home with no catch, his nets futile, trailing. Nothing changed. I'll help, she said. In days, she gave him a fine bolt of white silk. Spun while he fished, she said. Go sell this in the village, she told him. For a spell, his wife then fell ill. Still, as the fishing dried up again, she conjured a fresh bolt of silk.

Baffled, he lied, after a while: oh, the fishing had gone bad, he said. He feigned having left, but hid outside. In the hut, he found a molting, red-stippled bird, fighting to tug a quill from her side. It was his wife. Stop, he said, taking fright. But people will be denied the sight of a form-shifting bird; the gods, as forfeit, revoked his gift. Flying out, she cried, So long, husband.

"She's in pain, though," I said. "She bled on the silk."

"Why'd he forbid his wife from anything?"

"It's true," I said. "She kept him alive."

"Until he comes parading in."

"Telling her what to do."

"Can't even fish."

"So, let's edit it," I said. "She'll beg the gods to shape him into a bird. Paired, they'll go live in the wild."

"I love this tale, thank you." Lidija got up. She'd infused a jug of goji tea with a knot of apple mint, she said. Lidija brought me a glass. "Neil has herbs growing on the rooftop. Silas, this building's odd-job man, is paid to tend his pots. He brings me spoils."

I raised the glass, hiding my face. Neil had lent Lidija this loft. Its high walls, the split-level barre, latched in place. Part of the floor was sprung. Fitted to ballet, Lidija had said. "Is this the Neil you dated?" I asked.

It was. Oh, he just loved the ballet. He'd lent Lidija this place. Its walls used to be full of ballet images. But did Lidija get to look at the pictures I'd shot? "I think, Jin, hiding photos isn't suiting you," she said. "Next time, let's switch things up."

I did laugh at Lidija's habit of saying what she liked. But Neil's loft, with its sprung floors. His job in London. I had no right to ask. I'd push aside the figure of this Neil, his art. Next time, Lidija had said.

"Is that a yes?"

"Maybe," I said.

"Did you and Philip decide what you'll do, with children?"

"No." I kept thinking, I said, about Ives Joplin, an artist I loved. I'd cried, being let in a storied photo class Joplin taught. One night, he'd stated that half of us, the female portion, we'd all quit. Fated to begin families, we'd lose a fire vital to art, he thought. Joplin, thus, had not a living female artist he'd call a rival. Not, he'd add, for lacking inborn gifts. But the gift of talent, with its fire left unfed, died to nothing.

Joplin flicked to the next slide, having just told half of us we'd fail. He kept talking, this man I'd exalted, while I felt his insult shift, melting. Fluid, shining, it turned solid, mirific, a javelin pulling tall. I will be an artist you'll judge a rival, I thought, as Joplin spoke. In time, I'll do at least that much; I'll then go past you. One day, he'd find the javelin lodged in his throat.

"But if I did want a child, I'd have one, period," I said, to Lidija. Philip had typed a list of artist parents. Proving I'd work. The artists he'd cited also, often, hired a lot of help; still, none of this had a point. Not what Joplin said, not all of Philip's artists. I had friends who, longing for babies, wept each month they'd bled. Nothing, I said, might talk me out of desiring a child. "I also can't argue the urge into being."

"I'm with you," Lidija said. "It's foreign, this urge."

I finished the iced tea.

"Do you want more?" she asked.

"No."

"Should we begin?"

"I, ah—"

"Will you stand up, Jin? Don't move again. Not until I say you can."

⁎

Lidija hit me with a belt, over my clothing, while I braced against the wall. She'd asked, the last time, about limits, pursuits. I'd replied as I could. She'd given me a bell, its handle tied to a strip of tulle ribbon. Lidija twined the fabric in my fingers. If I let it fall, she'd stop. I kept the bell in my hand; I clasped it.

Back home, I went to the full-length mirror in the hall. I had slight marks, a pale flush radiating in lace tights. Philip had gone out. No, I didn't mind marks, I'd told Lidija. I'd make sure Philip didn't spot me naked tonight. Mild welts, veiled in nylon. I traced lifted edges. Injured muscles, elated. It had fit so ill, this rigid, vexing form. In which I might, at last, belong.

.

Philip had left out a large envelope from Chi. I tore it open, finding inside a print journal, the page dog-eared. It said that, with my triptychs, I vilified Christ's apostles. I had a violent, unique disdain for Jesus. I ripped the article, a polemic along the lines of what others had argued. Still, a poison; I shied it in the trash. I'd avoid the triptych photos, but I did, at last, open a cabinet in which I'd hid the kletic epistles to God. I'd kept a set. In what light could it project disdain? I began reading, face averted:

> Dear Lord, if You could, You'd recall how I fell
> in love with You. I was in junior high. Invited by
> a friend, I attended a youth-group revival. Used
> to the stained-glass hush of my parents' church,

with its chanting priest, ritual liturgies, I didn't expect such rejoicing. People hurling up bare arms, dancing. Jubilant, like disciples in the Bible, lit with split tongues of fire. I joined in the worship. O Lord, I leapt along on gale-force wind. I raged with fire, and yet I didn't burn.

I heard the front door's jingle, singing: Philip, home. "Jin," he called. Putting back the epistles, I ran to Philip. He'd slid on a heap of mail, then sat, in the hall. "People had Scotch," Philip said, his hands up. "Oh, no." I helped get him to bed. But, he added, they'd invest in his film. I high-fived Philip. I pulled off the left half of his pants. If I didn't, he'd get hot; Philip, though, tucked his legs. In a snarl of twill, he slept.

I'd work, I thought. But I waited. His tangled legs evoked a Philip I'd first known. I'd met Philip not long after I'd left the faith. I'd floated, grieving. I forgot to eat; I felt I'd thin to nothing. One night, panic broke through. Basic, plain truths had lied. Others might, as well. I had no logic for trusting that, taking a step, I'd walk, as usual, on this earth in spin. I could slip. I'd go flying. Sight whirled; I gasped, birds flailing in tight lungs. Kicking up dirt, shit. Stifled, I clung to a fence post. I wept, choking, thinking I'd die, as people called for help.

In the hospital, I was told I didn't risk dying. I'd talked of the earth's spin; I'd said I might be flung high. But I got lost in thought, afraid. If I'd catalog what I'd sight, I'd be fine. Using objects, I'd tie firm strings to earth again. Like this, the physician said, listing objects. He asked that I join him. I did; I exhaled, rough wings rasping. Birds crashed, flapped, escaping; I wiped soiled lips. Dirt settled. I pulled in a breath.

Panic lifting, I had to go home. I left, rushing, in a thin gown. I stole the hospital blanket, a wrap. I didn't walk long before I got stopped. It wasn't, though, a person from the hospital. He held an Edwards tote bag. Its beige fabric jutted with book edges. "I'm Philip," he said. "I just, I noticed you didn't put on shoes." Might he ask if I had far to go?

I said where I was going. Polite, he offered aid with calling a taxi. He tried until, giving up, he lent me his coat. Philip ripped his plaid scarf, fighting the cloth. Rolling halved strips, he devised felt slippers. He tied on strips. If I didn't mind, Philip said, he'd walk me home. I said yes, he could. Philip and I talked, the felt piling debris, twigs. Bits of junk, but I had tendrils coiling with each step, finding a grip on this earth.

16.

No, bitch, I'm not telling you my friend's name. Like I'd let that slip. Pah, I'll bust a gut. I'll shit my baji. I'd have made it through all right, if not for you life-spoiling Hans.

17

Can you tell me how you felt, after last time?" Lidija asked.

"No."

"But you're back."

"Yes."

Lidija put a kettle on to boil. "Jin, tell me what you're thinking."

I tried, but had soil filling in, peril. If I talked, I'd spit up the old, choking dirt. Not just with the risk of being thought ill, foul. If this dirt spilled, I'd open the hiding space. I'd let in a hope I might be found.

Lidija asked that I put both hands on the wall again. With a riding crop, she hit me until I replied.

•

Ice fell in a glass. "Hold it until the shaking ends," Lidija said. It would bring calm. She tipped puerh knots from a tin into cups; she lifted the piping kettle. I held the glass, ice rattling. Lidija, she'd helped me talk. I asked how she'd figured out what to do.

She laughed, giving me a cup. "Jin, I just listen."

·

Not a photo of Lidija was right. In the end, I handed her the open laptop, with all the pictures I'd taken. I walked to the loft's glass wall, staring out, as she tapped on the laptop pad. So, Lidija said. I wasn't using the shots?

"No," I said, turning. "But if you'd like to stop, Lidija, I get it. It's odd, for me, not having a plan. I'm trying shots. It might be for nothing."

"Injured, I have time." Lidija shut the laptop. "Jin, I love the pictures. No image is hostile. I'm not being rated. It's such a gift. The first time I posed for a ballet photo, I was told to strip, naked, so I did. No one said I had a right to refuse him."

·

"Did you buy the riding crop?"

"It's Neil's."

"He rides horses?"

"Yes."

"Is he still in London?"

"I have no idea. Let's stop talking about Neil."

•

But how well did I listen? She had time, while injured. Implied, then, a hint I'd ignore. Lidija might, in the future, have less time.

•

I pulled out the letters again. Just one, I thought. Just fucking read it.

> Dear made-up Lord, I lived in pursuit of You. Put me to use, I prayed. I'd long to be a saint. Lord, I'd go as You'd will, rapt, alone in the desert, singing of You. Give me the hot schist buckling, pebbles rolling, a patch of dirt lifting me to the sun. On high, from this stylite's column, I'd raise my hands to You. I aspired to the fanatic's striving, a life of undivided light.

•

I told Philip I'd kept taking photos of Lidija. I hadn't said what else I was doing, but I would. Until then, I had to see Lidija again. She traced a fading bruise on my thigh. I shivered. Philip, the past night, had noted the red spots; I clipped a side table, I'd replied. "Hasn't this healed yet?" Lidija asked. She patted a salving gel on thigh skin. I was lying across Lidija's lap. I had thought I'd be fine, not having this.

•

I shot Lidija tailoring ballet shoes. She ripped satin. "I'll be back to pointe in a bit," she said. Shell-pink ribbons fell through Lidija's fingers. She taped up the injured ankle. Using a folding knife, Lidija etched beige treads. Lidija, in splits, jotted notes on the ballet she'd stage. She raked tight limbs with a jade stone. Lidija at the barre, leg tall. Strong thigh sliding down, then rising again. She dipped; she lunged. Lidija put on a Libich string quartet. She'd explore its swing. In the glass loft, she carved air, space, in fresh lines. It was plain Lidija had to dance. She'd heard sylphs call; body replying, what could Lidija do but go along?

•

Often, while I shot, she'd talk. Did I not like working in film? I had, at first. But I'd wait so long for the image. With film, I had less control. She laughed. "Oh, of course," Lidija said. She asked why I'd switch reflecting panels. I taught Lidija the logic behind trading out a lens. She adjusted dials, fiddling with the focal length, as I'd gloss what each change did. I spoke of photos' lexicon. I shot; I'd capture. Film, loading. Image, seized. I had a life of targets. Photos adopted the idiom of guns, its brutal jargon still polluting the form.

Lidija, too, lived for an art defined by flag-plying men. Ballet hailed, in part, from a French king. Royal, opulent agitprop.

She talked about its Medici origins. Its past life as a kind of up-scale brothel. Rich patrons; ill-paid girls. Called, in Paris, pe-tits rats, the girls all but peddled to men in silk top hats. Or, well. Not quite past, the art form often, still, corrupt. But Lidija loved it, as I did image.

She and I, after I'd shot, might take up what I still called, even in my head, playing. If Philip had gone out, I'd then mix aperitifs, or she'd put on a pot of puerh tea. In spite of the first couple nights, Lidija didn't tend to indulge in alcohol. One glass, then she'd stop. It hurt the dancing, she said. Ordering in, we spoke, while red-gold light swept the loft.

•

Lidija had no habit of confiding. She'd jostled, all her life, with girls for roles, a rival surging in each friend. Plus, being first, set apart, hadn't let Lidija trust people with much. But I didn't jostle with Lidija. She'd talk as though, both of us held in a spell, the first night in Marin had gone on.

She told me of a Mr. Le Coq who hadn't loved Lidija's danc-ing. She'd just moved to New York. He'd scold Lidija, often. Baffling, for Lidija. Still, she'd trained to be quiet, obliged. Each chiding implied Lidija might be worth such effort. She'd push through. In a ballet studio, Lidija's body, her life, had to belong to the art. If, as she lifted a leg, the piano halted, she didn't bring it down. She held it high, while Mr. Le Coq, strolling to Lidija, noted that her leg was quaking. Lidija had no right to expect the public to buy tickets to watch if she didn't put all she had in ballet. She might as well go tap-dance in Japan. "Oh, the child's leg is falling," he said. "Useless girl, she's crying."

Lidija didn't object to his jibes. No more than did the soloist who, per ballet lore, had lost a top role after Mr. Le Coq, turning his ankle, broke it. Or the corps girl who kept erring, lifting the wrong, left fingers. He bit the right hand, in the hall. So that she didn't forget, he'd said. Lidija heard that, once, an irate Mr. Le Coq strode through a glass wall. Shards erupting, he didn't get cut. It was his wrath, people said. With Mr. Le Coq, glass will yield.

She toiled to do Mr. Le Coq's bidding. It was part of the job. Mr. Le Coq let Lidija drop, in class. No doubt, she'd failed again. But as Lidija twisted, pain firing, she felt afraid to stand. Mr. Le Coq had a shoe tip, shining with polish, an inch from Lidija's face.

"Did that hurt, Lidija, child?"

"No," she said.

"Will you quit?"

"No."

"Is the plan to tap-dance instead, child?"

"No."

"Get up, then," he said, so Lidija did. Days later, the pain still raged. Silent, Lidija kept dancing. She cadged other girls' pills. Mr. Le Coq then cast Lidija in a big part. She'd filled the job well, at last. In ballet, Lidija did as she was told.

"So, this, it's novel," Lidija said. But she liked playing this role. In fact, Lidija hadn't tired of it at all.

.

I'd told Philip we'd wait to talk about a child, but still, helpless, I brought it up.

"But why can't I be enough?" I asked.

"It's not about a lack," Philip said. "Jin, the world's burning. It's absurd, if—"

"I'm being absurd?"

"No." Philip clasped my hand to his chest, pleading. "Jin, I am."

The fight stalling, he said he'd love going to the fish shop. I asked for a bottle of wine, a Friuli. Seagulls dived, then glided. Philip, holding a sliced, net-tied lemon, baptized high-bellied oysters with squirts of juice. I nudged aside a plate of herring. "Not going to finish that?" he asked. Philip had a bite; he ate the rest. "Oh, no," Philip said, as he dabbed up the last bits of oiled dill from his plate. "I ate all the herring. How'd I get this full again? Oh, no."

I tipped into Philip, laughing. Friuli emptied, we paid the bill, and left, joining hands. Head on Philip's arm, I jolted with his steps. I can't let you go, I thought. If I tried to picture it, I failed. In each post-split afterlife: Philip, still there. He'd slip past, adept love. Quick-witted Philip, eluding the riddle of it not being a life I'd want, one in which I'm apart from him.

*

In truth, I had but shifting ties to the logical. I didn't have Philip's faith in a ruling usual. I'd begun in a God-fired crucible, dust flecks glinting with His touch. Devils stalked the night, thick-quilled plumage trailing. Rough, brush-tip tails flicked evil. But Christ held us close, divine aid being nigh. Saints' effigies fell open, spilling gilded tears. It was a faith I'd left, but I hadn't quite lost old habits. I still had a child's hope of, perhaps, shaping the world. Of tilting it as I'd will. I'd get what I want. If I'd just wish it enough.

*

During the fifth time, Lidija's ball gag was too big. It slid out; foiled, she added tape. She tied on a cloth, tripling the wrap. "It fits," Lidija said. I could yell, if I liked, though it might not be my call.

I then had drinks with Sahaj. It was before an opening, the bar loud. "Let's find a quiet place," he said. "Jin, the hell did you do last night?"

"Karaoke," I whispered.

"Did you shout all the songs?"

I had, for the most part, yes.

•

Still, I hadn't upended my life. I didn't ignite a thing. Not, for instance, like the Han who'd joined a high-school group resisting Japan's occupation. His parents, heroic, had blown up a bridge, killing foreign police. In love with a girl in his group, he'd talked, boasted, of his parents' exploits. It was rash. On a tip, the police had taken in this girl. She told police what she'd heard of the bridge. He, his siblings, and parents all died.

•

Each time we left the loft, people turned to catch sight of Lidija. Suitors trailed us, hailing Lidija with trite lines. Dazed gallants fell at Lidija's feet, tributes she ignored. Regal, she trod the bodies, like strewn petals. Lidija's startling grace had to help her win roles. More jostling, then.

But I'd be Lidija's friend. She'd alluded to one-night flings. Just with men, though. If, at Lidija's direction, I shed a skirt, it wasn't for long. Lidija and I didn't kiss. It was nothing like the old Han tales. I had, at most, a slight crush. It would pass; I felt, with Lidija, tranquil. It was only after I'd left Lidija that the longing began. So, I'd spend time with Lidija, this friend.

●

I gasped, fighting for a breath, until Lidija's belt went still. I'd told Lidija about the fits of panic. "Inhale," she said. "Hauling it in to the end. Jin, hold it. Exhale, as far as it'll go. Inhale. You'll be all right. Out, until it's all gone. Inhaling."

I followed Lidija's direction; the gasps ebbed. "I think I'm all right."

She laughed. "Like I said, Jin."

●

Lidija and I had rules in place. Offering the bell, she'd signal a role change. I did as she said as long as I had the bell in hand. If I broke a rule, or didn't listen to Lidija's bidding, I'd fail. But I hadn't learned yet where failing led. I didn't intend to let Lidija down. If I let the bell fall, or Lidija fetched it, we'd drop back to being friends again. In and out, we'd slip, form-shifting, equals, then lopsided.

●

I'd walk, often, shaded by a hat. Fires up north subsided. People filled the blocks, as in a festival, exulting in the pure light, rid of ash. Open faces, legs bared to the tops of swift thighs. I didn't have, in the past, a habit of casual lusting. It wasn't just that I'd loved Philip since Edwards; before him, I still hadn't felt the kind of quick urge friends did, desiring people walking past. Elise, for one, kept a rolling catalog of all the people she might find alluring. She'd predict, in a flash, who'd be single. Life with Hiju made Elise's skills less vital; it hadn't dulled this gift.

But as I'd stride, the prolific world rushed in. I had it, too, at last, this punch of longing. Pines surged up from tiles, bark spiraling. I'd walk, alive to the cyclist who held still, staring. Light-rail trains hurtled past, asphalt shaking as I did. I noticed the ink-florid person who, hipshot, sloped against a shop wall. Lilies arched fresh sepals, pistils fertile with gold dust. Oh, I thought, oh, so this is living. Nights, while Philip read scripts, I unlatched shut glass. I flung the sash open. Scents rippled through, estival wind singing of lust.

•

I brought Lidija all the tales I recalled. I found guides, in Hangul, to Korea's legends. With Lidija, I read out loud. But 엄마's tales, or so I kept finding, left the given paths.

One wife of legend, with a man fighting in a battle, lived on a cliff ledge. She'd just stand there, alert, waiting. Inert so long, she dried into a large, dutiful stone. I, though, had loved a myth of the wife who, tired of crying for a ship-captain husband, plunged in the sea to go to him. The gods, who prize daring, led this wife to his ship. She fought at his side. In the

end, the gods, at the pair's request, fused them in a megalith.
It's still on the ledge, a potent shrine. Pilgrims visit this spot,
for help with being strong.

*

I had a rapid uptick in hostile epistles. I hadn't loved God, people said. No, I'd lied; I proved this, having left. It's faith's
harsh, tidied logic, this witch-trial dip: being saved is final. In
refuting faith, I spurn that which can't be lost. So, I didn't serve
Him in the first place. I'd made it all up.

*

High-end shop bags often littered Lidija's kitchen. Fine, radiant cloth bristled in tissue-gilled depths. Lidija paid for all the
hansik we'd get in the loft. "Jin, I'm hosting," she'd insist. But
if I met Lidija out of the loft, she still paid. Once, at a bar, Lidija
slid the bell in my hand. "I'll get the bill," she said. She'd then
tip so well that people might dash after us, asking if she'd
erred. Lidija spent as if from spite; after a while, foxed, I let it
happen. If she'd like to talk, she will, I figured.

*

Dear Lord, I was in the high-school parking lot.
Friends talked of hearing You speak. I listened,
quiet, as jet clefts slit the earth. Slight cracks of

faith kept parting, each rift sinful, hot with Satan's patient breath. I can't help doubting You, Lord, I'd beg. In private, I called. Split this life for kindling. Set it alight, O Lord. Ignite this flesh, and still I'd run to You. I was pulled so tall with longing, a pyre of lust, that I thought You had to respond.

•

She'd had to fight with a boy in a ballet studio, in Dallas. Spoiled, he left pins in Lidija's shoes. He tripped girls, and shoved. Once, he ripped Lidija's tights in a spot she didn't notice until, mid-jump, she'd flashed the class. Kids laughed; the boy, most of all. He didn't hide his guilt. "Lidija, he's flirting," Miss Ilyin said. "He just has a crush."

Lidija heard the adult, a fool, and thought, Fine. She, Lidija, had to stop him. So, as he next pushed Lidija, she yelled. Miss Ilyin told both students to mop the studio. She felt let down, Miss Ilyin said, by Lidija's lack of will.

He lived close to the place, and biked; Lidija relied on a bus. Miss Ilyin left. Lidija waited. He wrung his mop in the pail; as he bent, she hit the boy's stomach. His head sluing down, Lidija's thigh shot up. He fell; his nose bled, its profile angled.

Lifting the boy's head, Lidija said his nose had broken. "But it's just cartilage," she said. Not all his parts fixed so well. "I'm holding back. Listen, you'll mop this place. It will be polished. No pranks, just dancing. Nod yes if you can do this."

His nods flecked Lidija's shirt with red pips. She left; he didn't hassle Lidija. In fact, he quit. "It wasn't a loss," Lidija said. "He didn't respect ballet. Insulting it, not caring. He was petted just for being male, willing to dance. Oh, well."

"He didn't tell people?"

"No," Lidija replied, smiling.

I tried not to watch Lidija's hands. Long, able fingers slid rope through a tie. Refining a knot. "Did he—"

"He didn't tell people a girl beat him up, no."

She'd tied five knots in a line, each bulge identical. "How'd he explain his nose?"

"He fell, cycling." Holding the rope to a light, Lidija said, "But I relived the fight. I'd think of his crying. Jin, I kept it, his shirt. I didn't wash it again. None of this felt right. I'd fret about being evil. So, to learn the high I felt, with him, might also be what people want—well." She tied a sixth knot, fingers nimble. "Now. Jin. Stand up."

•

I'd avoid pain, in general. Once, I sliced a palm on a catalog's edge. It bled for a while, hurting. I told Philip I might have to go to the hospital. I talked about its being, perhaps, infected.

No one alive had coped with such a pitiful cut. I caviled to Philip, Lidija, to friends. It closed; I forgot about it.

•

Ballet shaped Lidija's most trifling habits. Hips open, Lidija didn't stand in parallel. If a plastic bag flitted to the ground, she'd get it while halving, agile, folding at the waist. Or she'd balance on a leg, tilting forward, its pair lifting in a calm, lithe penché. Raising a leg in a split, she glided the limb straight up. Lidija lived as if part of an exalted line of being.

•

Close calls did happen. I was naked, after a bath, as the door hinged open. I shut it, swift, with a bruised leg.

"Jin?"

"I'll be right out," I called.

Philip said he'd be in the kitchen, fixing a salad. I dressed, hands jerking.

"Didn't you have lunch plans?" I asked, as I walked up to him.

"Hiju, but he's ill," he said, pouring oil. "It's tabouli, with feta. I added chili garlic. I figured you'd like a plate."

I held Philip's waist, from his side. "I'd love a plate," I said.

"Do you have to work?"

"I'll eat lunch with you first." I did kill the lights, before sex.

Still, I thought. If he got in while I was bathing. I'd had no idea Philip was home.

"Is this salted enough?"

I tasted his salad, its spiced, citric tang. "Not quite," I said.

Philip turned the salt mill. It was large, solid, hewn of pied cebil. Part of a gift from his uncle Juan. I put a hand to Philip's soft, trusting face. His full chin, the slope I prized. Philip tipped his head, nestling. Salt fell, bits of crystal, like sparks of light. I'd stop, with Lidija. I had to; when, though?

•

Lidija played ballet videos. Instep, she said. Line. On a stage, the fluted curtain is lifting. With it gone, this world opens. No one's hiding. Harsh lights; dust flaring as with a single breath. In this hush, she'd step forth, posing a question. Like a spirit facing the Lord.

•

One bride spilled a grain of rice. For this slip, whipped, she died. Rising in floral shape, with a bride's red lips, she'd haunt the living. But in the legend I'd heard, a brave, skilled girl hunts well. She dies while hunting, loved by all. Bereft, the people wail on this girl's burial soil. Until, at last, a red-lipped plant buds. People rejoice: it's the girl again, fresh with life.

"For a grain of rice," Lidija said.

Lidija and I talked of the shock we'd both had, finding out that, in the begats Korean families kept of births, with lists often going back centuries, girls' lines didn't exist. Just the sons. Until not long ago, girls had no rights. Quiet, a wife served. She might be exiled for failing to issue male heirs. Or for being loud. Simple talking could get a wife put out. With no place to go, jilted, she'd die.

It started that night, slight tendrils curling as Lidija and I spoke. So, people might think us abject, pliant. Docile objects. It soiled us, this defiling lie. But plied with dirt, I'd plant a garden. Or so it began, an idea coiling to the light.

·

Philip's oldest sister, Isabel, visited. I taught. Hiju's lab won a large grant, in physics. Up on Elise's rooftop, we fêted his triumph. I had an article publish. Philip and I paid a shiva call. I joined a picket line, a protest of oil funding art. Helen and Nhi, the friends living down the block, invited us to Ojai for a night. In Malibu, I gave a talk on the art of portraits. Philip signed a film deal. I had drinks with Elise, then Sahaj, all while I thought of Lidija, the real life I was hiding.

·

Dear Lord, late one night, in Noxhurst, wind blowing, a maple flinging down its fruits, I asked that You give me a sign. I'd tried to ignore the doubt, Lord. But ringed with cleft earth, I had no place left to step forward, not if You didn't help. I asked, and Lord, I—

I don't know how to tell You this. Each time I try, I fail. Lord, I asked for help, then I waited—

•

"It's a bad habit," Lidija said. I kept holding my breath to get through pain. "If you don't listen," she said. Lidija put a hand to my lips, nostrils closing tight. I was tied to Lidija's bed posts. Before long, quick light forked. I fought the stifling hand; at last, she let go. "So, you'll listen."

Late that night, alone, I looked it up. People didn't advise choking. It was high-risk playing. I hadn't said I'd be fine with being choked. If I asked that Lidija not do it again, she'd stop. Once, she'd hit me with the explicit object of forcing me to drop a bell. Proving I could, Lidija had said, as I flung the bell down. I'd bring it up, the choking. But in the past, I'd given no thought to being choked. It hadn't figured as a hope. With that night, it did.

•

Idle spells, hours, that Lidija filled as liquid spills in a gap. I forgot what I'd thought of, before this. Ballet having much of Lidija's time, she didn't want texts, calls. I held a phone, thinking of Lidija, hand wet with the grip. But I'd mind Lidija's rule. If I didn't, the phone might slip. It could take Lidija along.

18.

THE KISAENG'S STORY, AS TOLD TO JIN HAN

I plotted. I'd known all along just what I was: a kisaeng, slid-ing on the margin. Reviled, but I ate well, lolling in bed with slip-skin grapes. Not eligible to talk with noble girls, the prim little cunts, but I had a tip-top mind. I was caged; I ran wild. It's jail, for a girl, being a wife, while I'd get to rove through town in fine silk, flashing jade, taking in sights. I didn't belong with the whores, not quite, but if a rich old dipshit asked me to his bed, did I not go lie with him, prating, Oh, it's like a drag-on's tail, oh, how will I fit it in?

So, I made plans. I'd find a place; a tavern, perhaps, for us to run. It's a cinch, talking people into doing as you like. It's akin to all seducing: just reflect back the person he'd love to be. I'd get the funding. I had a patron list going.

19.

I'd felt, until Lidija, that I kept a rigid schedule. I lived serving the art, I thought. But next to Lidija, I lazed. I reposed. In New York, she'd paced a five-block radius. She'd go to ballet, then home. Once, while on stage, she broke a big toe; the part had Lidija jump up and down, in place, hard, as if on knife tips. But Lidija didn't stop dancing, the pain driving through. Injured, Lidija still lived in a spin of ballet. Up at six, she trained with straps, bands. She danced prone, legs ticking, like time stalling. "If you'd call this shit dancing," she said. Lidija had drills, weights to lift. It was dull, insipid; diligent, she did it all.

She also had a ballet to stage. Lidija played film of her own past self, still dancing. She wept, taking notes; face blotted, she'd watch the film again. Lidija hadn't yet hit upon what she'd stage, but she would.

I did ask, at last, why I'd found so few clips online of Lidija's ballet.

"Oh, bah. I just didn't like there being casual videos of my dancing. Bad lights, tinkling music. I hired legal help to get those erased."

I nudged plastic lids open, the hot broth of kalbi tang oiled red. She sliced the kalbi in thin strips, ribs piling. I told Lidija about photos I'd taken the spring after I left God. I focused, I said, on a cult at Edwards, the college I'd attended. People in Jejah, this cult, had blown up abortion clinics. One person, Phoebe Lin, was said to have jumped in the Hudson, and died. But people also thought she'd lived. She'd feigned death, perhaps, then fled.

Lin, though, had planted a bomb killing a group of Noxhurst high-school kids. Not by intent; Jejah didn't set out to kill. But five people died. Before Jejah, Lin had friends, a life. I staged photos as a Lin who hadn't joined a cult. I had props, outfits. Using makeup, I aged my face, giving this Lin a long, pacific life.

I'd shown the project to a friend, Elise. She asked if I'd thought of the people who'd loved Lin, had known Jejah cultists. It was just a couple years ago; Lin's class hadn't yet left Edwards. I hadn't thought of it, at all. With the final exhibit closing in, I pulled the Lin images. I rushed to trade in a figure of Korea's past, a Samil activist the police had killed in 1919.

None of it held up to the Lin photos. It was the right thing to do. I had a poet friend, Sahaj. Julian, Sahaj's husband, did happen to be Lin's friend. Old photos of Lin often depicted Julian, his arm tight around Lin. He still left the table, upset, if people spoke of cults. I didn't like the idea of facing Julian if I'd revived, in public, his lost friend.

Lidija folded a napkin. "I," she said. "Well."

"You what?"

"Not saying it's right, but . . ."

"Go on."

"I'd have shown the first set of photos."

*

I failed to bring up the choking. In truth, I had no desire to object. Not if Lidija didn't.

*

Notes from Baptists kept trickling in. People hoped I'd die, that I'd be raped. I tried to forget the notes.

*

> Dear Lord I made up, I'll try this again. More
> faults slit open in earth's frail crust, the gaps di-
> viding. I tried eluding its cracks. Don't let me go,
> I prayed. But late one night, in Noxhurst, dirt

shifted again. I put out a hand, to a maple trunk. Its rough bark solid, I lifted my eyes, at last, to felled buildings. Ruin, debris, being all I had of a life I'd thought I'd give to You. Earth split, dirt blowing. I tripped on the path. Face down, I pled for a sign. Maple limbs flung in high wind. Slight winged fruits, soft as flesh, filled open palms. Rising, I had foliage clinging to shirt cloth, maple fruits I held. I swept it off, and left.

O Lord, I didn't ask again. For so long, I'd thought, If I fell, I'd slip into a rift. But I had it wrong. Instead, I fell, then what I had pitch out of sight was all hope of finding You.

·

One man had a gift, a parcel. Magic flesh, he was told. Cut from a part-fish girl's tail. If he ate it, he'd gain infinite life. He locked it up, afraid. Such gifts cost high. His child, packing, about to be wed, ate this flesh. She'd thought it plain fish, but woke up opal-hued, like a fish twirling in full light. Men fell in love, right and left; this urge proved fatal. Each man died after a night in her bed. People talked; the word circled. Do not go to bed with the fabled, shining part-fish. Still, men kept falling in love. She had to take flight. Isolated, she'd repent, living on as a famed poet.

"Is this tale your mother's?" Lidija asked.

"The part about being a poet is hers. In the original, she just hides."

"Did she have to repent?"

"Oh, since—"

"It's not her fault," Lidija said.

"People did tell the men to watch out."

"Still chasing this girl."

"It could get old, the one-night stands."

But, Lidija noted, men died of loving this part-fish. Not all beings did. She loved, perhaps, a coeval part-fish. One who'd also dined on magic flesh. It might be hard, though, eluding male pursuit. So, in time, they'd dive to find a sunken, aquatic citadel, the place hectic with spangled kin. It's built of pearl, shell-lined, the banquet halls paved with hadal drift glass. Legs fill out as tails. Still a poet, she'd sing to the fish-people. Epic ballads of life on shore, distant as ship hulls on high, floating along.

*

"Do I get to meet this new friend?" Philip asked.

"Who?"

"Lidija. It's as though she's not real."

"Well, you met in June, at Irving's."

"I don't think I said a word to Lidija."

"Didn't you?"

"No."

One Han told a friend he'd go live with a film starlet half his age. He loved this girl, he said. But he had a child with his existing wife. On the night of the fire, just his wife was home, the child with his wife's parents. He died, while he slept; she lived. No one thought she'd killed him. She was upright. So filial, people said. It had to be the kisaeng's spirit again.

Lidija asked if I'd give her photos I didn't plan on using. Not just to have, though. For Lidija to use. In public, even, perhaps. She'd begun thinking of what she'd do after ballet. It could help, having more of a high profile. She might post ballet images, talking with fans. "But if you hate this idea, Jin, I'll drop it," Lidija said.

People, I'd read, often had to retire from ballet before thirty. Lidija, then, had five years left. Obliged to attend a talk on post-ballet options, she'd jotted down a short list of jobs suiting dancers. Jewel design, talent agent. Modeling, acting. Journalist. Insulting, Lidija felt, to the listed jobs. She knew nothing of jewel design. Still, she'd framed this list, hanging it on a wall. It helped Lidija's dancing if she kept in mind that, in fact, life ends after ballet.

But she'd plan for this afterlife. Riding abrupt hope, its upswing, I said, "Let's do it." Maybe Lidija and I, we'd go on as friends, helping each other's work, until—

No, I'd quit there, at until, I thought.

"I'll edit options," I said. "I'll bring discards. But take the image credit."

.

"I used to think it odd," I said. She, the kisaeng, had died along with a first-born Han, the son. His parents, not hers, had foiled this couple. But in each sequel of the alleged curse, it was just the girl spirit's fault. Once, as an adult, I'd asked. Hostile spirits, I was told, used to be thought female. One idea being that, if a girl died ill-used, she'd lived pining for a reprisal long denied. Ditto, with a wife, such being the roles possible, back then, girl or wife. People felt disquiet: this rage, pent up, might find a place to go.

.

"Let me tag along tonight," Lidija said. I had a local artists' gathering, at a pub, to host. But Elise had said she might be going. On the night Elise first met Philip, while I still thought him a friend, she'd had the inkling I'd date him. With Philip, I relaxed. It's as though you're finding a home, she'd said. I didn't want Elise talking with Lidija.

"It's just for visual artists," I said.

Lidija didn't push. But when I got up, she said to finish the radish soup.

"I'm going to be late," I said, then I was being pulled back, topknot in Lidija's grip.

She asked if it could be right, to disdain radish soup. Staple of hansik, noble plant. In harsh times, it kept people from starving. Bad, prodigal girl. It was Lidija's fault, though. She hadn't kept me in line.

"I have to go," I said.

But with Lidija's breath singing along hot skin, I forgot the usual guilt. I'd skip the pub night. With a slight push, a laugh, she sighed. "Go, all right." Still, Lidija's point was made. Pitted against a clock, a pledge, she'd triumph.

        Dear riling Lord, I left for exile. In this novel place, I shied from people; I hadn't known of being so alone. Nights, I'd climb to the Point. On its ridge, I'd admire the world You left behind. Gusting wind ripped white mist, strips lifting, ribbons that open skies. Do you see it yet, Lord, what You miss, having died?

•

I'd brought Lidija a pint of Beldi olives, as a gift. She opened it; an oil drop fell. Lidija asked that I wipe the spill.

"I'll get a napkin," I said, puzzled, but willing.

"No, Jin," she said. "Lick up the mess."

She flipped the box. Oil-bathed olives rolled pell-mell. I got down; I hadn't licked a spill before. Not even with Lidija, but I jerked forward. She'd hit me with a riding crop. I put a hand on olive skin. It split open, the oil sliding.

"Such a mess," Lidija said. "Oh, well. Eat it all, Jin. I want shining tiles."

I moved fast, crop flashing if I let the pace slip. I lapped flecked trails of oil; I ate the olives, rich salt filling my mouth. Lidija had out a tall bag of black currants. She spilled the fruit, as well. I picked those up. I had one job, pleasing Lidija.

"I wish you'd see this. Up," Lidija said.

She led me to the ballet mirrors, a wall of rail-sliced glass. Ordered to spin, I did.

"It's as if you've come in from the wild," she said.

I was bright with oil, juice-stippled. Legs shaking, I did look wild. Not fit, as I'd fretted, for public living. But I'd leapt past shame to a fresh, unruled place. I didn't care, at last, if I'd belong. Instead, I got to be this.

·

I was still elated as I got home that night. Philip had taken a trip to Isabel's, in New Haven. I had the urge to go out. In the hall glass, I caught sight of a wild-haired being, flicking past. Halting, I sidled out of my dress. I unfurled, florid with big, lush bruises. Petal hues; juice stain. I'd spring colors, life, from pain. I was thinking, at first, just of holding the sight. If I had a picture, I might not forget this self in the glass. One with a figure, this place of lifelong shame, that also held a garden. I tried phone shots, but the hall light was dim. It subdued the image; I tried again, in the studio, with a tripod. Pulling down the backdrop, I used a fill light. But in the photos, colors dulled. I looked pitiable, like a battered girl.

I might turn literal, I thought. Paint could help. I rifled cabinets, but I had just half-spent, dried oil tubes from an ill-fated attempt to add paint to images of relics. I'd require silicone; art shops had closed.

But the late-night deli would be open; I ran out. I found cuttings: daylilies, gladioli. I bought six pails' worth, all the deli had. Jared, the clerk, asked if I'd like him to wrap the cuttings. "No," I said. I bore the plants, dripping, home. It still not being enough, I went to a stripe of dirt by the building. Up top, it was pale, arid, but I dug until I hit thick, black soil. I heaped it all in a pail. Inside again, I spread dirt on studio boards; I tore gladioli. No one's watching, I thought, as I ripped petals. It's just you. I stripped. On the ground, I piled soil, gladioli, and lilies on top of my skin. I posed inquiries while I shot.

So, what did it feel like, being hit? Rude shocks, heat; the insult of pain. I'd lust to fight back. But then, I'd give in, and Philip, I wish I'd told you how it felt to stop caring. Often, in people's bodies, force bred. It begat the malign, to pass it along. I, though, refined pain as delight. In the injured place, I flo-resced. I'd open petals from evil.

I kept taking photos. Birds chirping, I rolled up shades. I lifted a sash. Mild, dappled light filled the studio, foliage shifting. I shot again. Stalks, fibrils, pushed flicking through slats. Peti-oles rippled; fresh buds, unfolding. Leaf-tip tendrils frilled, to spiral mirific along solid legs. Not possible, I thought, with the light-tattered rags of what I still had of an I, to love a calling this much. It's a gift lacking all parallel, being trusted with so full a life. Once, I had to go into exile. I was told I'd find noth-ing past the walls, but look at this gain.

*

I slept, then woke naked, shivering. Rinsing dirt, I got in bed. No, I thought, bolting to the studio. I pulled up the images that, last night, had felt alive. I, lolling on a hip, legs angled, heaped with petals. Sight lines pointed to part-veiled, colorful slips of flesh. I, flushing with dawn chill, residing in a first, unspoiled shape. In the halo of each photo, I had no trope to elude. I didn't flout a heritage of the subject odalisque, a reclining nude. Male sight lost its rule. Inside this garden, I'd act as I will.

•

I edited images; I set the phone's alarm. It pinged before Philip's flight. I left for the airport. In the car, he put his palm on my thigh, a nail hitching on the denim stitch line. I stroked the top of his hand.

"Do you want sushi?" I asked.

"I'm craving the laziji at—"

"Oh, let's do that."

"Unless you're set on—"

"No, we'll get Sichuan," I said.

I tasted it again, the delight I had, giving Philip what he'd want. But if I didn't like the idea of Sichuan, he'd be glad to have sushi. Or we'd get both, as take-out. He'd plate the laziji, a stir-fried knoll, nigiri in a spiral. I'd put on, at his request, a tango vinyl; we'd duet along.

I'd said I'd go with Philip to Isabel's. But on the night before this trip, as we ate, I'd had a sharp, abrupt thought. I tried to push it down. Philip's parents; his sisters. His cousins, flying in. It was a close group, with Philip, the last-born, still indulged. Isabel might bake rogel cake, using the Selig recipe Philip loved. His uncle Juan, halloing, toting in a vintage Malbec he'd saved:

he'd open it for Philip to taste. In this blithe Selig chaos, I'd put up a façade, posing as Philip's wife, both of us all right, thriving. I didn't have the acting skills to get on the flight.

I told Philip that a large Selig gathering felt too hard.

But I'd already said I'd go, he replied. I'd let down, of all people, Isabel. Selig elders. Isabel's girls. "Is it, Jin, I didn't tell Isabel. No one will press you—"

"Philip, that's not it."

"But . . ."

"I can't tell if you thought about it, Philip, in depth. If you'd want a child."

Philip slid back from the table, his chair's legs rasping. "So, it's why you won't go to Isabel's."

"It isn't," I said. "But I tried to be upfront. If people didn't insist I'll be a parent, I'd have no idea of it being a life to avoid. I also don't plan to go live in the Pacific fucking Ocean. It's that foreign. I kept saying this."

"I want a child, Jin. Most people do."

"Not all," I said. "Sahaj thinks he won't." Lidija, too, I thought. She'd heard tales of giving birth. Hips split; torqued ribs. Spinal injuries. Mangled pelvis. People who'd stop ballet, hanging up a life's work. One fetus had jutted a leg through his lining. He'd lived; his mother, a soloist Lidija admired, had died.

"But I did give it thought," Philip said. "I felt I'd be fine, not having kids."

"Fine?"

"I just, Jin, I had you."

"Don't you, still? Philip, I'm here."

Philip and I, as if caged, paced the old fight. Its walled, tight logic: his aching, the ghost child. Urging, then refusal. Philip yelled. I fled again, in a panic, to the hall closet. Philip, giving in, said all right. Just a trip. He'd talk to Isabel, the girls. Jin had work, he'd tell Seligs.

•

"It's odd, though," I'd said, to Lidija. Such high rage, leveled at people like us. Not from Philip. But so often, refusing to have a child upset people. Selfish, they'd call it. The pope, a celibate, thought it depraved. People disputed the idea. No one had argued with Philip.

"It's a threat," Lidija said. "It's still, as a life path, distinct. Implied is the fact I'm picking this, not that. People start asking, So, what else might this bitch think of doing? Jin, imagine if I had a child, but kept dancing. The jerks, they'd still be pissed. I'd be called unfit, a bad parent. Or if I did give birth, then quit ballet, I'd be judged for staying home. Bigots die mad."

•

Philip ordered the chili-oil fish soup, laziji. Noise drifted from the open-plan kitchen. Its sizzling loud, a prelude. No, like a ballet crowd: fast, light claps, hailing the soloist's first spin. It's all just begun. Image hadn't left. Next time, I thought. I'd add props. Spectacle. I'd work again; I had that, as spoils. Riches with no equal. Philip ladled a top level of chilis off the fish soup's golden broth.

"It's hot," he said. "You've been up all night."

"What?"

"You're jittering."

"No, I slept."

"For, what, an hour?"

Less, I thought. If the photos didn't have to be kept from Philip, I'd tell him, in detail, of last night's glories. Jolted, at first, with shock, he'd turn to reveling. He'd invite friends to our place. In high spirits, he'd set corks to popping.

"I had projects to grade," I said. But I'd go wash my hands. Out of sight in a stall, I cried. I'd had a decade to confide in Philip. Instead, afraid, I'd lived in hiding. I'd given him a partial Jin. Philip, I might have let you run.

20.

THE KISAENG'S STORY, AS TOLD TO JIN HAN

But the plans I'd made got all fucked up, with the culprit being, oh, right, a bigshot Han. She'd had a fight with him, but didn't tell me shit. No, I'd pitch a fit, she said. I'd be mad, then I'd get us both killed. But he'd gone on a trip. I pled for details. One didn't fight with a noble prick. She refused, but did admit that, upon his return, he might still be upset.

I ran to the head kisaeng. If my friend got hurt, I said, I'd light the house on fire. I'd bring the fucking place down. In days, the head finagled help from a high-ranking noble living in Seoul. He loved my friend's singing. She'd join his home, to be all but a third wife. Rich, this noble, but my friend declined. Not while I stayed. I had a quick tongue; I picked stupid fights. If she left, she'd be unable to help me at all.

Go, I said. I'll be fine. But she kept saying no.

21.

I'd tied gladioli spires with a snip of flax. I gave it to Lidija. Portraits, I said, the late-night deli. Its floral pails, hints of flesh. I'd kept the night's work; I had photo ideas. Lidija held a fist to her open mouth.

"Jin, you did it."

"Not in the past tense, I—"

"Right, I get it. I'll fend off the jinx." Lidija tapped a divan leg with a toe.

"But if I hadn't shot pictures of you, I. Lidija, you helped. I, ah. I'd have no photos, I think, if not for you."

"No," she said. Lidija tilted back in a long stretch, tight shirt gliding up. "It's all you, Jin. But I'll help again."

·

I left with time to go to a florist, Osip, on the next block. Lidija knew the florist. His shop, she'd noted, had lavish bouquets.

"Osip, please treat Jin well," she said, calling him, slicking balm on my wrists. I'd chafed skin, fighting Lidija's rope bind.

In his shop, the florist asked what I pictured. Lush, I said; profuse. Osip sold me piles of hibiscus, lupin. Peonies falling with each step. I had to be driven home. Philip was there; I asked for a hand getting it all inside.

"It's for work," I said. "I can't talk about it yet."

His eyes wide, Philip fell silent. I'd have to figure out what I'd tell him. But tonight, I had no time. I shot portraits in a froth of petals. Ballet had taught me to be precise, explicit, with posing. I'd fretted while taking in life's gifts. It felt as if living, all of it, had led to just this night, bending to each photo. I didn't stop working until, vision blurring, I tottered off to bed. I had fresh images again.

Since I'd tried so long to abjure who I am, I staged tableaus of altering form. I plied lichen-hued argil; I twisted foliage. Lidija plaited jute, twigs, and drift glass in a tall bird's nest. Once I'd patch-dyed ostrich-egg shards, I shot. With the help of a wild-bird refuge, I bought a heap of molt peacock quills, which Lidija sewed in plumed, curving horns. I tinted skin opal-blue. Paint still wet, I added swirls of quills. I shot, taking flight. I gilded plume tips. Gold spilled on the studio boards, to open slits of light. In a thrift shop, I found tangled angel's wings Lidija filled out with ripped lace, a swath of tulle. Sequins, a bridal veil.

Hanji chaplet. I thought of the ailing crane, pulling silk as she bled. I draped rope netting; I let injured flesh shine through.

I sent Lidija discard ballet images I'd edited. "Use them as you like," I said. I asked a friend to let us into an Oakland dance space, late at night. It had a past life as an old light depot, with model lamps still pendent from its ceiling, unlit. Plush, tattered couches ringed the stage. People would sit there, plunged like jewels in split cushions. But that night, I was alone with Lidija. Not quite able to jump, she said, but she'd get there. I shot Lidija upon the black stage; filming, also, at her request. Lidija whirling, the pale shoe a candle's wick. She spun like a high flame, a twist of signal will.

.

I didn't ask what I might be doing. Not, that is, past the circling frame of each image. I'd fill, in private, I thought, an abiding lack. I craved a pledge others had from birth. Philip, you had it, as well. Idle couples stroll past. People kiss in line at the café. Pop ballads sing of a boy who longs like you. In ads, tabloids, the Bible, top-forties songs, people like you exist. It's a surfeit of public, trivial signs you'll stand tall, taking pride in who you can't help being. I'd tried ruling it enough, the pining. It's also a kind of living, I thought, to desire. No less full, intact, for being stifled. But Philip, I did want more.

•

Long hair wild until Lidija held it in a fist, a leash she pulled high. I was tied in Lidija's flax rope. Paradigm of the girl in distress, but I'd adapt the role. Instead, daedal, I played the escape artist: I leapt to hope. Ignited nerves fired pleasure along each line of rope; I was tied in light. I'd turn the abject into gold.

•

If I had a sip of tea, I'd fiddle with the cup's handle. Its glass like the pure, calm line of Lidija's throat. I'd pick up a marble evoking the ball of Lidija's wrist. It hurt to sit; I thought, Lidija. I'd floss, and I'd recall Lidija's hands adjusting a gag. Legs buckling, I'd grip the basin. It furled through me, this longing. Each time it opened, large wings flailed to rip me apart.

I still met Lidija once, perhaps twice, a week. If not working, I'd tend to be with Philip. He rang the bell, holding a box of Fuji apples; I lunged, to let him in. I read Philip a script, giving him pliers as he fixed a broken sink. He jarred plums Sahaj foraged. Oil-drum asados on Elise's and Hiju's rooftop. Sunday idylls with 1960s heist films, Philip's head lazing in my lap as I fed him figs. I'd plotted a life with Philip; he had my time, but Lidija, she lived spotlit.

*

Dear vexing Lord, can I tell You, though, what it is to push on living while I don't have You? Its strength, Lord, this urge, the cut-stalk lust to persist. Lopped free of afterlife, of everlasting, I dangle bare legs above oblivion. People topple in; I will, too. O far-flung Lord, You won't stop the fall. One artist, not long before his death, noticed a lilac sprig by his hospital bed. He'd marvel at the lilac, still pulling water from its slim vase. Dying, it drinks, he said. It goes on swilling.

*

Philip, as a rule, didn't walk in the studio before a loud rap: calling, he'd wait. But that night, with Libich quartets playing, the wind high, I heard nothing. I jumped at Philip's touch.

"How'd I wake up alone?" he asked.

"It's work," I said.

I was editing a heap of drift glass. Philip went rigid. "You're editing?"

I nodded.

"But this is a photo?"

I said yes. "I have to work," I said, with a laugh.

His palms flaring, Philip backed out. Drift glass, I thought, pulse fast. It had no lock, the studio; I'd work in quiet. Philip said, as I slid in bed, that we'd go to Jinju. Opulent, a six-top. Prices ran high; I tried not to want it often.

"It's late, to get in," I said.

"I just got a couple of seats," he said. "I pulled strings."

"*What* strings?"

"I get things done."

In Jinju, we had kelp-twined squid. I'd put on a long silk dress. Chili-spiced crab. Basil kimchi. Philip fiddled with the dress strap; he'd strip it off, at home, he said. Quince kalbi with pickled garlic. Jebi churi in rich kaenip oil. I'd turn the lights off, first. Quail kimbap. Litchi tarts with candied pignoli. Philip praised Jinju to the chef, with brio; she handed us both a glass of tokaji, gratis.

If I'd shot at Jinju, I'd have images of mirth, of clinking flutes of sun-gold tokaji, thin stems glinting. Philip tells a joke; laughing, I spill a drop of tokaji. It pearls on silk. Philip blots it with a kiss. I didn't want this night to end; no image holds it still. Not a thing to do but live through its spell, nibbling litchi, then to let it go.

·

Philip, I still thought I'd be right back. Lidija might be called to New York in the fall. The ballet she'd stage was finding its profile. If I tried to think past the fall, I'd stop there, at if. I hadn't yet tilted at ruin. Not like the Han who, in high school, fell in love with a girl his age. Eloping, the couple fled north. It was going to be a swift trip, a jaunt, but this was in 1950; war irrupted. It was said they'd died trying to get back, though it was hard to be sure. No one heard from the couple again.

.

I was up late, editing, when a slight draft spun past. But I had the studio blinds shut; drafts didn't get in. It edged along, this odd chill. I heard, I thought, a sidling hiss. I was just tired: I hadn't slept well. Still, I got up. In the hiss, I'd heard, perhaps, spite.

Philip had gone to Miami on a work trip. I thought of the jesa rituals I'd known, as a child, festival offerings put out for spirits. Not apt, but I did have joss sticks; half-joking, I lit the tips. It was late, in Miami, or I'd call Philip. I might go to a hotel. Instead, with the faint hope of lulling this spirit's ill will, I filled a plate with fruit: a Fuji apple, jujubes, dates. I placed it on the desk.

I left the studio; in bed, I kept the lights on all night. "Don't be a child," I said, out loud, bird matins trilling, as I crept in the studio. I raised a blind: strong light sifted in. Joss sticks had fallen to piled ash. Nothing else had changed. But as I put the offering, a jackleg gift, back in the kitchen, I felt soft flesh on the Fuji apple. It had a large, dark spot, the fruit pulp until its skin. I probed the spot; damp, it slit open, issuing a malic tang. I'd have noticed it, last night. No, but fruit did spoil. It had just shown up, though, as if with a spirit, avid, taking a bite.

•

Chi called. He'd talked to Nigel, who'd said I still had yet to divulge a thing. It'd help if I'd give Chi an idea of what I was up to.

"Chi, I'm not—"

"It's just that, Jin, you're the last artist holding out."

"I don't—"

"Nigel's willing to beg."

"I'm taking, well, it's a self-portrait cycle. It's the, ah, Ovidian idea that form-shifting begins with a trial. Pain so large it can't be held in one's existing figure. I'll adapt Korean myth, though. Not Ovid's. I'm altering the origin tales."

"I love it, Jin," Chi said. He'd tell Nigel. Ending Chi's call, I shied the phone. It glided, rattling, as I clung to the desk apron. I was still playing with ideas, a student, the night a collage artist said I'd like talking with Chi Qiu, a gallerist. I'd hosted a studio visit with Chi; he'd stayed in touch until I had photos fit for showing. Chi didn't forget. It had to be why I'd told him, to prop open the gate. So that, in time, he'd get inside.

•

Dear Lord, I'm still not saying it right. Not lopped, not dangling. I didn't let go, Lord, of this loss. No, one night, You fell in the pit, a gash cut in dirt. Since then, I've sat at its lip. Lord, I've kept vigil. Others I've lost, the people I love, join You in this cleft. But I'm still the child told I won't lose a single person, not with You to guard us. I perch at the gap. O Lord, I watch for You.

•

Lidija and I met at a dive joint; I got there first. I'd failed to eat, but I had pili nuts in my bag. I'd rushed to get shells for a fishtail. It had taken a while, finding the right kind. I'd left a thirty-gallon trash bag of mussel shells in the tub, packed with ice. Lidija was late. I didn't mind. Hip-hop purled from the jukebox. I licked salted pili oil. I'd taste the waiting.

Lidija sat, leg jolting up, down. She'd left a linen shirt lapel tucked, its fold bent. Not like Lidija, being less than poised. But just as I noticed, she'd also begun going quiet, the agile spine rising. She stilled the jerking leg. Regal again, tranquil, Lidija said, "I had a call. I'm upset. No, it's fine. I'm a little on edge. I'll forget it. Let's talk about you, Jin."

Fishtail, the shops, I said. Jet beads; cattails. I'd made

lilliput-shell bangles. Lidija fidgeted, nails tapping. I asked, "It won't help to talk about this call?"

"No, but I'm not upset. Let's go on talking about you. It's helping."

I did as Lidija said. It was like the first night, though one-sided. Lidija asked; I replied. Drink spent, she got a refill. I told Lidija what, before I left social media, I'd loved. It was the self-flaunting, I said. People who'd post bold pictures, bids for praise, a dollop of lust, which they'd get. Photos of a lithe figure upright in a fitted, thigh-slit gown. Dipping in a lake. Parading elan, a slice of leg. I found it elating, I said. Nephilim of style. Posing, radiant. It felt like such an open, giving part of life. People calling, Do you see me? Others replied, with delight. I'm here. I do.

Not long after this, Lidija asked what I kept in mind during an orgasm.

I paused. I said I didn't; if I had to sleep, I might, but as a last option.

"It's a last option?"

"It has a high price. Of guilt. It's absurd, though. I'm failing us, but—"

"Who's us?"

"Oh, women," I said.

"*All* women?"

"It's disloyal."

"To women?"

"Well, to feminism."

"You're failing all women, plus feminism, with this guilt," Lidija said.

"Go ahead, laugh. But yes, that's how it's felt."

In spite of what I'd said, Lidija hadn't smiled. "Jin, you're agitated."

"No," I said. I had, again, a single job: she'd asked to be diverted. "It's nothing."

"Don't lie, please, Jin."

I tried to explain what I'd told Chi. "He'll, Chi—"

I halted, throat closing. Lidija asked for a glass of ice. Items lining the bar's wall: fading tote bags. Pint-glass spire. Oil painting of a top-hatted marlin. Nevada license plates. Edison light strings, picric, dim. One sign, lollipop-red, listing well prices. I held a tulip glass, ice tinkling. Panic ebbed; I sipped melting ice.

"Oh, Jin. It's the photos?"

"I didn't plan on telling Chi."

"You think—"

"Chi. Philip. I can't let Philip, well. I won't exhibit a thing. I can't. It's just what people expect, that I'll be servile, quiet. I'll add to the china-doll trope. It gets us killed. Lidija, I'm taking its part, just by—"

In hiding, I'd had a refuge. But rash, flouting all the rules,

I'd dared go out. I had no place to hide; I'd ripped up the haven. Go, I thought. Run. But I was tangled in filth, shit, and I had rifts to hop, clefts gaping, the ruins sliding in. Red sign, top-hatted fish, tote bags. But with a tilting earth, the listed objects slip in. Only the birds will rise, trying to escape. I won't; I'm in this trap. I might lose Philip, I thought. People stared; the cue-ball pock stilled. It's the mob, turning. Lidija helped me back to the loft.

"I'm being selfish," I said, through gasps. "You're the one who's upset."

"No. Stop. I stirred this up. I have an idea, though." Lidija hit me a long time, hard, until I let the bell jingle, falling. Lidija held me as I cried; the panic had broken. "I'm here," she said. "Jin, you're all right. I'm not going. I'll figure it out with you. I'm right here."

22.

I had no time for arguing. I paid a shaman to help. She called on spirits, howled, spun, the old shebang.

Oh, she said. I had a path to the ending I'd want. But I'd give up the kind of living I'd known.

Sure, fine, I said. So, tell me what I'm doing.

But it was all she'd pass along. If I'd just listen to the wind, she said.

23.

I had a card, postal mail. In its tight, coiled script, this card said I'd die. Its front image: a plain, faded U.S. flag. Laid on top, an invoking scroll. *In God we trust*, it lied. I hefted it, this first threat I got at home. I put a match to its tip, holding the card above the toilet. It ignited with a lick of gas-blue flame. Chi was right; with people like this, I had nothing to explain.

Dear Lord in whom I don't believe, I woke up furious. I burn with the parts that can't be said: haven't I envied others' tangible losses? I covet the palpable dead, Lord, of a kind with relics to give the living. Objects to touch; graves to tend. Bodies, Lord, while I'm left with nothing for a shrine, just this life, shaped by longing. O signal illusion, I'm blown like glass circling a God-sized hole; shaved thin, I turn people into light. Harsh ghost, for all I ask, You don't visit in a single dream. Not once, but still I'm made to cling. O Lord, will You not let me go?

•

Philip said I should invite Lidija to our place. He'd ask Nhi, plus Helen. I'd said Lidija liked olives; Philip had his salt cod recipe. Maybe he'd add tarts, folding in tío Juan's nduja.

Nhi said they'd love being with us. Both had to cancel, though, ill. I left a get-well bag with Nhi; I trudged home. I'd tried to figure out who I could invite, this late, with hours to go. Sahaj was in Palm Springs with Julian. Elise, no; Hiju, at his lab. I didn't want Lidija with us alone.

Up the steps, then I called hello to Philip.

•

"Let's sit on the front porch," I said. Passing a bottle of Trepat cava, froth spilling, Philip, Lidija, and I talked. Philip said I'd shown him a clip of Lidija's dancing. He'd thought it a sight. It was a thrill, having Lidija Jung with us.

Lidija thanked him. She spoke with Philip of the Teatro Colón's glories. I let the bottle pass; an elm leaf glided on

Lidija's head. Last night, at Philip's request, I'd shown him a clip of Lidija's dancing. He'd said that, alas, ballet wasn't for him. I'd heard Philip reviling his debt-piled place of origin for the fortune it had spent, updating the Colón. He relied on slight fibs to be kind, a host. But not with Lidija, I thought.

Lidija smiled, though; she'd had a role, last June, dancing at the Colón. "I played a nymph," she said, while a gust of wind parted elm foliage. Light shot through. In its slant glare, an image stirred. Lidija tipped back her face, the elm's laurel clinging. It felt, for an instant, as if I'd kept it all whole. Lidija, Philip, and I sit talking. Cava spills. Spindrift floats, perlage rising; a high wind lifts. Folded wings unfurl. Set each quill to rippling. Spin it into flight, and let's all go on. But the wind lapsed. Rustling, the elm stilled. In fading light, Philip said we had no cava left.

Inside, Philip carried his olive-infused nduja tarts to the dining table. I brought out a Rioja that Philip and I first tasted years ago, in Spain, where he picked me up after I'd traipsed half the path to a shrine of the apostle St. James. I was still taking dull shots of objects. I'd funded part of this trip through a grant. Pilgrims sang; pining, I hiked along. Each night, I salved blisters. I slept in public hostels, too fatigued to ask what I hoped to find in Spain.

But in Galicia, Philip had flown in. I left pilgrims behind to drive with Philip, his advent a jolt of life, mirth. Philip blasted oldies singing of love; I fed us piquillo chilis. In Rioja, I finagled a visit to a small, fabled vineyard. It was run by the Trejos, jovial triplets. Showing us the place, they'd tippled on Trejo wine. The eldest triplet let a bottle slip. It broke, red wine squirting his ironed pants. "Listen, a spill brings luck," he'd said. "Bah, he's full of shit," the third sibling had said. "It's just that he drops a lot of bottles."

Philip brought home taped cases of the triplets' Rioja, far past the legal alcohol limit. He lied at the airport, being asked what all his boxes held. "Olive oil," he replied. The official, with a sigh, said to go through.

"So, if the official did open a box?" Lidija asked.

"I'd have paid the import duties," Philip said.

"I travel, often, for ballet," she said. "If I'm caught lying, I'll be flagged."

I glanced at Lidija, her angled face calm.

"Is that true?" Philip asked.

"It is. I can't lie to a federal agent. It's not from principle."

"It's hardly a risk."

"No, I'd be on edge. If I had the Rioja, he'd notice I'm lying."

"I have a friend, Julian, who'd gone to Madrid," I said. "He put a leg of ham in his bag. Julian was held up for ten hours. He lost the leg. I think he is, in fact, flagged. Julian still rues Hidalgo as though he lost a beloved pet. Hidalgo's his name for the Iberian pig's ghost. He baptized it, this pig's leg. But I'd guess a risk like that isn't going to jibe well with ballet touring."

I had both Lidija and Philip laughing. Ballet plans did run tight, she said. Philip fetched hot plates of salt cod. Lidija did, as he'd figured, love the dish. Philip had just produced a film taking place at the 1992 Spain Olympics. He'd heard of a group of Olympics athletes polled as to what they'd do if given a half-decade of first-place wins, after which they'd be killed. Most said they'd accept the bargain. "I'd take it," Lidija said. I began relaxing.

Next, Philip brought up a short film he'd viewed. It depicted a person dancing ballet on a piano lid. But with knives laced, tip down, to her soles. She flailed, knife points etching the lid. In pain, hollering with each step. Philip still thought about it, often. Had Lidija tried this kind of ballet?

"No," Lidija said.

"It was striking," he said.

"Philip, will you get the port Isabel sent?" I asked.

"I'm sure it is," Lidija said. "But it isn't ballet."

"She had on pointe shoes," he said.

"Or I'll get the—"

"I don't let people see that I'm in pain," Lidija said. "I might call it a first rule. People will go to class with a leg in a full cast, toe to hip. If I'm hollering, it isn't ballet. It might be art. But it's just not ballet."

"Isn't this, well. Jin thinks I should shut up. Not long ago, didn't ballet include just white people—"

"Philip," I said.

"—the logic being that others didn't look right," he said.

"I'm not talking about racism in ballet with a white man," Lidija said.

"I am not white. I was born Felipe, in Buenos—"

"But you'd pass as being white. It helps you lie at borders, Philip Selig. I'd be afraid."

"Seligs fought Nazis," he said. "If it's what you're asking."

"No, this isn't what I'm saying."

"I didn't pick being Philip. I tried to change it back to Felipe, but I was a kid. Still, I do get it. In grade school, if I got caught talking in Spanish, I had to write lines, 'I will speak English,' on the board. But you didn't begin life as Lidija with a *j*. How much did you hope to be white, to take up 'Lidija' as a child?"

"Philip. Stop. Philip, what is this?" I said, at last.

"It's still Felipe on my passport."

"He's not in his right mind," I said, to Lidija.

Lidija rose, head lifting tall. "I'll go, but thank you both. I ate well. Philip, I'm glad we spoke."

She left, the latch bolt clicking. I asked Philip to explain what he'd said.

"I don't, Jin, it wasn't the plan."

"It just, what, slipped out, asking Lidija why she'd aspired to be white?"

"I thought she implied that Seligs——"

"But she didn't," I said.

"I felt like the help. Lidija didn't ask me a single thing. If I had a friend who——"

"If?"

"Right, no," Philip said. "I've had male guests treat you like the help."

It leapt to sight, flicking past, a line of people, men, who'd slight a wife. One film mogul had broken a side lamp, then let me, Philip's wife, get napkins. I'd knelt; I wiped the shards, while he went on prating, as if he had nothing to do with the glass. But I swept this spectral line aside. Philip didn't invite those people again; it wasn't part of a fight. "I'm polite, though, hosting. I don't insult a guest."

"But this Lidija, what is she to you?"

"She's a friend, helping me work. One who might, after tonight, stop."

"I didn't set out to insult Lidija," Philip said, his voice surging.

"I'm asking, Philip, that you not yell."

"I love that knife-dancing film."

"Lidija's danced with a broken toe. She had to jump on it, still, as if on a knife tip. But didn't I tell you this? Philip, will—"

"No. Oh, so I'm insulting Lidija on purpose, is that it? I don't fucking think—"

I got up. Philip's chair fell; he came with me, down the hall. I put on a jacket.

"I'll write Lidija a note," Philip said. "Jin, what are you doing?"

"I'm going to check if she's all right. Don't wait up." For the first time in a life with Philip, I left.

24.

On the night I'd paid a visit to the shaman, I paced the garden. I had to finish living as I'd known it, she'd said. I'd then help my friend. "But doing what, spirit bitch?" I asked, out loud. I paced, but I heard nothing. Just the magpies, calling.

It was late for magpies to be up. I found the birds perched on a wall. One hopped down, its stiff tail ruffling. It piped, a hello.

Often, I fed scraps to the birds. I'd fought the dipshit kisaeng who, long ago, with a stick, had pelted a magpie. It broke his wing. Insolent pest, she'd said, but magpies don't forget. It got to be a feud, the whole flock diving at this dipshit's head. She had a little girl, one she kept inside. Still, the birds swept in, biting the child. Pah, the little girl lost an eye. Dipshit pled, at last, to be moved, with the girl. But like I said, she'd invited the fight.

Oh, I thought. In a gust, the flock left.

25.

I broke a rule, calling Lidija. She picked up. I'd had a fight
with Philip, I said. He'd had no right to talk to Lidija as he
did. I'd left home, upset. I had places I could go, but if—

"I'm on the bridge, going to Marin," Lidija said. "Irving's in
Palm Springs. He lent me his friend's place. If you want, join
me there."

.

Moths lining the front wall flicked porch light. Chips of gold, I
thought, old gilt flaking off an icon. I held back, unable to ring
the bell; I was the pilgrim at a temple, edging close, then shy-
ing, but the door swung open.

"I kept watch for you," she said.

Lidija faced me, backlit, splendid. I forgot what I'd thought
of saying.

"I find that I talk a lot about gin, the drink," she said. "On a date, I'll have a gin fizz, hibiscus gin, Sapphire, gin on the rocks. I talk about oil-lamp djinns. Jinxes. Hijinks. Jingles. I fit that word in my life. Jin. I didn't figure out what I was doing, at first. But after a while, I did. Jin, you show up. I'm here waiting. It's as if—"

She paused. "It's as if what?" I said. "Lidija, finish what you're saying."

"Will you tell me if I'm alone in this?"

I lifted Lidija's hand; I kissed strong fingers. She pulled back. I'd erred, I thought, but Lidija's mouth, lips wide, lapped mine. I fought Lidija's dress, trying to find a latch, a placket, to let me in. I hit, at last, a ridge to slide open.

With a step to the side, Lidija said, "I left the candles lit, up in the turret."

I followed Lidija. In the high-walled turret, tall candles' light flitted in glass depths. I undid the pale dress. It fell, circling Lidija's abused feet, the striped cloth a halo. Light dulled, abrupt, the candles blowing out. No, I thought. It was Lidija: she'd eclipsed the rest of sight, making it all blind spot.

"I, it's not a first, being with a girl," I said. "Not since Philip, though."

"I'll tell you."

"If you don't mind."

Lidija's full laugh pealed, ringing the turret like a large bell. "Jin, I love telling you what to do."

"I'm on my period."

"So am I," she said, taking off my shirt. I trailed the path down Lidija's taut skin, licking slight hairs in flames. She guided fingers. Do this. Oh, like that. Lidija's thighs, pliant flesh. Shaved quills, fine bristles, tossed sparks. Salt liquid; a rich, metal tang. Like melting gold, I thought, but Lidija pulled me up. "Legs wide," she said.

"It's not worth the guilt."

Lidija placed a hand on my mouth. "Such a bad girl," she said. Losing control, with base urges. But I had Lidija to help right the wrong. I let tight legs open. She kept talking, hand gliding in, until I was shaking.

Once I'd gone still, she left. I drifted; Lidija fetched wine, along with a slim folding knife. She hinged its blade. In the quiet, she held the tip to a candle. Lidija asked if I'd hold out the arm I'd burned, in college, with friends. She nudged the fading wrist spot. "It's time to update this, I think, don't you?"

Lidija waited, knife willing, poised. I might elicit details, I thought. Or refuse, but I'd slued past caring. I said yes. It flashed, then again. Sight blazed, pain-bright: I leapt back. She'd put the knife's flat, its tip, to the old spot. Parallel sides, half-ogival, rising. Like wings, I thought. Idle words, floating.

Lidija left the turret. She applied a balm, fingers light, to the fresh, pulsing burn.

*

"Jin, I picked the fight. Philip sat with you, hosting. It felt hard, not being him. But I wasn't kind."

"It was Philip, too," I said. Or no, I thought. It's a single person's doing. Not Philip's, nor Lidija's. Hiding, I'd lied to Philip. But I'd lost guilt's coil; let it wait. Patient, it always did. Lidija had draped a lithe, solid arm, shining with life, on my leg. I had a sip of wine. I licked dried lips, tasting iron. "Is my face red?" I asked.

"Get up," Lidija said. I did. "Spin." Lidija's eyes glinted, the light fitful, but I wasn't afraid. In all this time, she'd kept me safe. "You're like a wild thing at a kill," Lidija said. "Stained in triumph."

I got out the camera I had in my bag. "Is this all right?" I asked.

"Not my face, but go ahead."

"It won't be public. I just want the image, to have."

"Make it public," Lidija said. She didn't mind. I shot Lidija's leg slung on a length of thigh. She swept the fluid we'd bled along a hip. Lidija, inking as I shot: line, pip, and spiral. "If periods were judged male," she said. No one would hide it, this sign of being virile. Of pain defied, a badge. It would bring pride, the fact of having bled.

•

In New York, Lidija had gone to a first ballet gala. She was a student, then, a child, still growing. One man spoke to Lidija. No one else had talked to girl Lidija all night. His full name, Neil Heyl, topped playbills. It gilded the building walls. He inquired, polite, obliging, about Lidija's ballet hopes. She felt less out of place, like an adult. He joked; she laughed. Neil, fifty-one, invited Lidija home. She'd just gotten, in Dallas, that spring, a driving permit. Indigent, she lived with him, but hid the pairing. No public outings. Lidija stole in his building, through a side exit. It was her life, for years. People would think Neil helped Lidija with roles.

"But people found out," Lidija said. "It was so abrupt, like a wall going up."

Others thought Lidija cold. Invited to parties, Lidija declined. She didn't go to bars. But Lidija was just, for a while, broke. She kept it quiet, not willing to be pitied. In short, Lidija had no allies. Josip, the principal who'd drop Lidija, often pled for a date. She said no; jesting, he'd beg again. People then heard about Neil; Josip avoided Lidija. Until, that is, Lidija's final pas de deux.

"Once I fell, Josip, his shock, the cries for help: I, bah. His idea of a prank, I think. He figured I'd jump back up. But Josip's arm. I felt it go soft. Josip did let it fold."

"Lidija."

In the hospital, she railed that she'd quit ballet. Neil urged Lidija to wait. She'd find it dull, just healing. Didn't she hope to make ballets? Neil could help Lidija with a place in a top workshop, in San Francisco. Neil had a loft there, large, with a barre. She'd live alone; he wasn't going to visit. Lidija might use it as long as she liked. Lidija, addled, let him take her on a trip. On its last night, she told Neil she had to stop dating him, period. Neil didn't argue. But his loft, he kept at Lidija's disposal. So, here Lidija was, using Neil's place, healing.

"Jin, after I fell, I heard people laugh. I might be filling in that part. I hope I am. But I listen to it, at night. Devils, cackling as I wail. I can't decide if I'll go back to New York. If I do, I'll be with Thijs, Josip, all the devils. It's not as though I'd go public with this shit. It's bad enough as it is. I'd have Neil tied to my name as long as I'm dancing ballet."

"Lidija, if—"

"Before Josip let me drop, I also told Neil I'd stop living with him. Neil didn't object. But Jin, the other night, Josip put up photos of being at a club with Thijs, plus Neil. I had no idea they'd spoken, at all. Did Neil tell Josip I lived with him out of, what, pique? On that last trip, I still had trouble walking. Neil hired a private aide. I can't figure it out. Maybe Neil thought he'd clip his caged bird's wings. Or he didn't tell Josip. Still, I'm the girl who let Neil Heyl in my life."

"But you were a child," I said.

"I'd give up a lot, for ballet. Neil, at his first ballet, felt life's veil rip open. It laid him open to living. It felt like divine grace, he's said. Neil's a shit, but it did help, his love of ballet. Injured leg aside, I might do it all again."

•

"But let's forget Neil, tonight," Lidija said. She left, again. Stirred, the candles' light bent; a flame spit. It jumped high, roaring. Lidija's sole parent had died in this period, as she met Neil. He'd invited a child, isolated, orphan, to live with him. Rage wasn't going to help Lidija, though. Quell it, then. Fire settling, Lidija and I talked.

•

Lidija had to ask. She kept thinking of the tale I'd told, on that first night, of a kisaeng. If she'd adapt it, so that the kisaeng loves a girl. Might this be a fable Lidija could stage? In a private ballet, just with the workshop. One girl, a noble's child, is told she'll wed a rich son. It's not an option, refusing. So, the girls climb a pine. Rope tied, the girls leap. But the lovers' bodies thin, arch, sprout feathers, and split open, in wings.

Jute knots slip, the girls taking flight. Pairing for life, as birds. In crane shape, Lidija added. I'd inspired Lidija, with the photos I'd staged. "If you tell me to stop, though, I will," she said.

I had to tell Lidija no. Stop, I thought. But with lips to Lidija's fist, I let a kiss fill the quiet. Lidija, who'd revived dying photos. I had living pictures, again. She'd pushed a stone, lifting the dead. Such a gift, which I hadn't repaid. Lidija, who'd led me along still waters. I said to give me a little time.

"Of course," Lidija replied. She'd wait.

●

It got late. I'd lain down, drifting. On sight's edge, a slip flashed past. Slight, the hiss, but plain. I sat up. Lidija slept, a palm hiding her face. It could just be a draft.

Or, I thought, the spirit. Once, a first son fell in love with a kisaeng; as she, caged bird, prized him. Rash, this jinxed couple spoke at night, finding refuge behind a tall pine. Plotting a joint life, full of hope. So, let the idyll run long. If this kisaeng did visit, tonight, I'd invite the spirit in.

●

Up before Lidija, I woke to high glass flaring, cuts of festal light. Shards of beryl; jacinth, lapis lazuli. Iris agate, pied lines shifting. Lidija's hair rayed out, the lush, rich black tipped gold. It had, as she'd said, grown fast. Naked legs twined like sapling limbs, the bled-upon spots clotted rubies. In the garden of God, we'd stroll through jewels. One pale flame still burning, I put it out.

26.

He, this Han noble, had taken his trip south. Not even I could get to him. His petted sons, though, hadn't left. I knew the first Han son; his name, I forget. Let's call him High-hat. I sent a quick note, saying I'd just finished a sijo. In truth, I added, if he'd permit me to be bold, I'd thought of him while writing. Oh, he'd inspired the poem. Did High-hat plan to visit, that night? Do, I urged. I'd love to sing it to him.

27.

I sat in the kitchen, at home, thinking of what I'd tell Philip. Out of sight, dogs snarled, fighting. "Stop," a person said, as the light-rail train jingled. Fine ash lined the sill; I wiped it, thinking, Oh, god, the urge vestigial. I left off the capital, His title nothing, a long habit. I didn't ask God for help. I hadn't since the final night I'd tried, in Noxhurst, in a swirl of maple fruits. Pride, as I've said, is bracing. Even with the triptych letters to God, I didn't invoke Him. I'd made, at best, epitaphs. But I did want guiding. Oh, god, I thought, with the hours whirling past.

·

I had a call, from abroad; I picked up.

"Jin아, listen. 엄마 is ill. She's in the hospital."

Not quite awake, I asked 아버지 what he was saying.

"On Jeju Island, a flash storm. She slid off the hiking path. I ran for help. But she hit her head, falling down a slope. 엄마 isn't in pain. I'm at the hospital, in Seoul. She'll be all right. But Jin아, she's hoping you'll join us."

I told him I'd get a flight. I called Philip, who said he'd find plane tickets. In the hospital; ill. I rolled out a bag, then put in a shirt. I forgot what I was doing. If I aligned the timing. I'd had parents hiking in Jeju while I was with Lidija. Philip rushed in. I'd sat, with the bag. It still held just a shirt. "I'm packing," I said.

"I'll pack for us. I got midnight flights to Seoul. It's the first plane out."

"You're coming?"

"I'm going with you," Philip said.

"But you have that event, coming up."

"I'll tell them I can't be here, Jin."

"No, don't skip it," I said. I'd go to Seoul first. Philip balked. I insisted; he filled the bag. Head shaking, he said fine, all right. I didn't add that it might bring upset: Philip, with me. Philip made lentil soup. I had no appetite.

"Jin, I was out of line last night, with Lidija," he said, driving.

Last night, I thought. Philip and I, we'd had a fight. I'd

stayed in Marin; I woke to jewel light. It was the past. I'd left it behind. But for Philip's sake, turn back. Rioja triplets, a pig's leg. Knife-point dancing. He'd high-tailed it, to his office, before I got home. Philip still hadn't asked that I explain.

"I was a jackass—"

"Lidija was talking," I said. "It got late. I fell asleep."

"Oh, I figured. You had to help a friend."

Philip's pitch had shifted, as it did while I had a fit of panic. No, but with a change: Philip held back his own fright. If he'd left the house as I did, I'd fall apart. I'd begun lying to him about Lidija in June. Last night hadn't split, much, from things I did in Neil's loft. Lidija's not just a friend, I thought. I'd betrayed Philip all along.

He parked, lifting out the bag. It was here, the guilt, tolling. Its crash so loud, I had trouble hearing. I clung to Philip. But I had to get to Seoul.

•

She'd slid off a path, during a flash storm. It was swift, evident timing. I didn't object to Lidija's ballet. During a first night with just Lidija, I'd invited the ghost in my life. On the plane, I toiled to pull in a breath. Shale's rasp, gliding in thin, dividing panels. I choked, birds rising again, the dirt. But I had no right to panic; for once, I'd will it down. I ignored signs, then, in Jeju, she'd had a fall.

•

In the hospital, I was told to go to the fifth level. 엄마's bed had its top half tipped up. She had a white strip binding her head. I'd tried to be quiet. But she'd heard steps; face bright, she held out a hand.

"Jin아," she said, and I ran to her side.

28.

If I do the wind's bidding, will my friend go to Seoul? I asked.

Oh, well, you'll get that, the shaman said.

Tell me what you're holding back.

You'll be split from this friend as long as she's still living.

But after that?

It's not for me to tell you.

Is anyone going to tell me?

No.

If I don't do this, then what?

She might die.

Pah, I said. So, not a high price.

It's for you to decide.

I asked for a love potion. I paid, the phial in hand. High-hat
said he'd visit that night.

29

It was trifling, a slight jolt to her head. She'd told the hospital to let her go. Such a long flight. I'd gone to all this trouble. "But I'm so glad you did. Oh, Jin아. 아버지's fetching lunch. I think you'll like the soup."

So, I was 엄마's child; she, the host. I'd paid a simple visit. No time having lapsed, I had a stage role to uphold. He arrived, toting a laden, padded bag. Silent, he clasped me, his grip firm. She spoke of triptychs I'd shown. I replied, smiling if she did. He pulled tins from the bag, still quiet. I helped set the bed table with plates. I'd known him to be quick to hold forth. On politics, Korea's past, its glories: he'd get loud, agitated, with the pride of exile. But I played along. I had sips of broth. Spin the lie. If I didn't, I might break a spell. I'd lose all this again.

●

I'd stay at my parents' house, I figured. It was what he'd expect. But then, I said I'd go to a hotel; he didn't protest.

In the hotel, that night, I called Philip. "How is she?" he asked, on the first ring.

I told him. Hospital, I said. Its fifth level, for patients in bad, critical shape. On the flight, I'd read articles, studied graphs; I'd dug into head injuries. It didn't sound trifling. "Philip, it's as if the fight didn't happen. My father's being quiet."

"He's *quiet?*"

I laughed, then, also, I was crying. I had the hospital records. Did Philip—

"Itzel?"

"Yes."

He'd ask his high-school friend, Itzel Gil, for an opinion.

●

I was in the hotel bed, phone in hand, as it lit up. Itzel could talk, Philip said.

Itzel had the hospital's scans. Inside, she'd bled, Itzel said. If it did stop, she'd be, in full, all right. It did often stop. If it didn't, well, it might turn fatal. No, I just had to wait.

So, this shed light on 아버지's quiet. She might be dying.

"Rest will help," Itzel said. "But I'll urge you to spend this time well."

•

I got out of bed. I didn't belong in this place, a hotel. Its hush, the wide, pristine bed. I'd go to the hospital. But the clerk didn't let me sign in. I had to wait, it being long past the hospital's fifth-level visiting hours. I might, I thought, with the pen I held, knife the clerk's eye. I'd be put in jail, though, of no use at all. If I shoved past, they'd find me.

Back at the hotel, I cried in hard, fast gasps; I stifled the crying. I studied head injuries. I packed clothing. Jeju, a path; hiking, she fell. I added gifts: the catalog of triptychs, a coral silk twill wrap I'd bought for the wedding. Suiting, I'd thought, 엄마's hanbok. She still hadn't said Philip's name. I'd take the wrap.

•

I'd push guilt to the side. Let it wait, again; I'd first get 엄마 out of this hospital.

•

She'd sat up, alert. I'd ask for a cot, I said. I spoke with the head nurse; I cajoled. It did go against fifth-level rules. But I laid out plain logic. I could help, I said. I got the hospital cot. I sat with 엄마, talking, until she let slip that she hadn't quite slept through a night. It was, oh, head pain. It wasn't a big deal. On Itzel's advice, I had the pain-killing dosage upped. In the cot, that night, I held still.

She asked, "Jin아?" No, she wasn't in pain. She might read, if she could. But the light then kept her up.

So, I recited psalms; lulled, she slept. I hadn't lost a single line. I'd tried, in the past, to quiet His word. His dirge, updraft of spent love, rising as if with spite from depths His going left open. It often felt as though, calling down the pit to God, asking for Him, I'd just rustled up a loud, willful echo. One I hated, this pulse of futile song, its wraith's lilt outliving Him. But at last, it might be useful. If it helped, I didn't regret a thing.

30.

I sat with High-hat; all night, I poured his soju. On his fifth drink, I tipped a phial in his glass. I sang him a sijo I'd jotted that evening. He loved being with me, High-hat said, as I helped him, lurching, from the house. I might be the top poet in the land. In fact, I ought to be his wife. It wasn't a joke, he said. High-hat was asking. I said I would; he left me with his hat tie, a long string of jade.

I got my friend up. High-hat is taking me as his wife, I said. I pulled out his jade string. But if she didn't go, I'd refuse him. I held my friend as she wept. Pah, I said, it's not a parting. I'll find you. In just days, she left for Seoul.

31.

She slept often. If she was up, we talked. I shot pictures of the fine, strong profile. Oval shape, temples full. Slim nostrils, lips parting to laugh. Skin like oiled hanji filtering milk light. In the first roll I'd shot, I'd taken nothing but photos of this face I loved. Ill-lit, lopsided photos, lacking all skill. I'd thought it odd. It wasn't just being a child. She'd kept photos filed, dated, in spiral albums. I had, with the next roll of film, a close-up shot of a finch bathing, the image defined, framed well. But in the hospital, as I shot still more bad photos, I figured out this riddle. Image sluing, I forgot optical rules. I tilted angles, each photo rakish. Ring it with light flare. Spoil the image, but I'd find the sight ideal.

·

She asked, so I talked, confiding, again. But I left out what might upset the invalid. I tried to forget the long silence.

Nothing about faith. She'd have read that, in public, I'd spoken of being out; I didn't bring it up. No alluding to a kisaeng's ghost. "Is Philip well?" she asked. I replied as if we'd talked of him all along. Did I think he'd visit Seoul? Oh, in just days. She'd be out of the hospital, she hoped. If Philip liked kalbi, she had a place in mind. His first night in Seoul, we'd go.

●

I'd held it in as long as I could. But I did ask, at last, about living in Seoul. Not telling me, the only child. I'd heard it from a college friend of hers, a gallerist.

"It's 아버지's job," she said. In Seoul, he got paid well. She'd tried hiding the full picture of hardship, so that I didn't fret. Or, God forbid, drop the art. Still, I'd heard part of it. Ups, downs. "I wish I'd told you, Jin, darling," she said. "I was going to, but—"

"No, it's all right," I said.

"I kept paying for the old phone, and had it ring through."

"It isn't—"

"In case you called."

●

She spoke, after this, of 아버지's quiet. He'd sit jabbing at his laptop, still girded in a formal suit, his shirt fitted, crisp. But he didn't go in his office. Placing a work call, he'd step out, to the asphalt. I'd watch him, from above, as he paced, vibrant, his stride long. I'd marvel at his altering. Inside: tight, pallid, quiet. Outside: tall, unfolding. She sent him to get lunch.

"It helps him to walk," she said. "He's felt pent up, in the hospital. It's just that he's afraid. I'm telling him to have faith. He thinks I'm not facing the risk. Jin, I am. I'm praying hard. So, with God's help, I'll be fine."

•

"In Jeju," I said. "엄마, your fall. It wasn't his doing, right?"

She'd reclined; with a start, she sat upright. "No, darling. He isn't losing control. It ended, long ago, as I've said."

"It's not him, though."

"Oh, Jin. People change. Jin아, he didn't do a thing."

•

I didn't tell you, Philip, what male shouting calls up. If, as a child, I was told I'd bring police, the state, with talking. If so, I still might not be equal to telling it but, perhaps, in fiction. Conjure a girl, then, with parents born to a war-split land. It might take a while to adapt to how else people live. If he'd erupt, pitching his wife to foreign earth, hollering. Plates could drop. Flesh might gash. But if he was also, often, a fond, giving parent. If this child kept in mind the violent past, she'd forgive him. Not his fault, she'd think; he'd gone through so much. But if the girl, able to quiet his rage, rushed to calm him. She might begin to think she, alone, could quell earth's shaking. Not, perhaps, each time, though. If, for a while, the child failed to put an end to his fits. It might help to claim the guilt. So that she'd be able to stop the next time. If all this did happen.

*

I asked from which hiking trail she'd fallen. It was a peak on Jeju. Shaped like a crane, people said. Its name paid tribute to a girl who, pushed from the top, had died. I held in the panic. Once 엄마 fell asleep, I stared at the ceiling. Lidija's ballet; paired birds lifting from the pine. But here, large cranes glided in depths of inlaid pearl, darted spotlit along a coin. It was a bird people loved. So, it didn't have to be a sign. If it did, though. I ran this spiral all night, tight circles of if, then. Faint, thin light edged the blinds. On the flight, I'd sent Lidija a short note. I'd had to take a trip to Seoul; "I'll explain when I can," I'd said. But I'd stop the ballet. I'll give Lidija up, I thought. I'll do anything.

*

She asked that I go back to church. Not a single time, but as part of life. "Jin아, faith isn't willed. It's a profit of ritual, the habit of worship. It's like what you do with photos, darling. If I have one hope, it's this. Jin아, will you go to church?"

It was the fifth night. I'd upset her if I refused. Since the flight, I hadn't slept. I'd fetch juk, ice; I'd open blinds, reciting psalms. I didn't quite exist, at this point, as a self apart. I'd flung off a dividing skin. Instead, writhing, alive, I had this sole, elating grail: I'd get 엄마 out of the hospital. Plus, Jeju; the spirit I'd flouted. First, I'd help her rest. I'd fix the lie after the hospital.

"I'll go to church," I said.

"You will?"

"But you'll have to live such a long time, busting all the records. You'll be 이혜진, a legend."

"Jin아, oh. Oh, I feel so light. I lack nothing."

•

But perhaps, giving in, I let a vital string go lax. It began that night, 엄마's dying. I'd left the hospital. I had to wash, I thought. In the hotel, I hustled, but not enough. I got back to high-pitched alarms, people circling her bed.

I ran in, then I was being pulled out. I flailed. It was a nurse; I pushed. I kicked, wild, until I got in, at last. But she'd slid to a place of no hope. Still, I pled, asking that she wake up. 아버지, crying, bid God for help. She lived a full night past the doctors' odds. I knew, though, what she'd be doing. She'd fight to get back, to give us a less abrupt ending.

In the end, I said it was all right to go. I knelt at the bed, kissing 엄마's still, quiet face. He wept, holding us both. I said she'd given me a life I loved. She'd led me up to this point, guiding me well. I'd find a path forward. If she had to go, we'd get through it. I said we'd be just fine. With the light rising, she died.

32.

THE KISAENG'S STORY, AS TOLD TO JIN HAN

High-hat told his parents he'd take a kisaeng for a wife. No, his parents said. Nobles like him didn't wed girls, filth, like me. He left. Finding me, High-hat said I'd be his wife. Let's go live up north, he said.

33

O n the night after she'd died, Philip got in to Seoul. He held me tight, choking with tears, hot fluid spilling. I felt it as a relief to quiet Philip. I hadn't cried since the hospital. She'd left me a note, signed in red ink, with a dojang. I didn't open it; I tucked it in my bag. I'd go, with Philip, to the funeral hall.

·

엄마 was put in the earth. Philip had thought to bring formal high heels. I tilted forward, on toe tips. If I forgot, thin lifts bit through soil, the lapse like skin tearing. People in bell-shaped hanboks left. 아버지 bent; he placed his fingers, gentle, in dirt. His lips moved, silent. I had the urge to tell him I'd, perhaps, stirred up a kisaeng's spirit.

But he'd rush to dispel fright. I'd be selfish, telling him. No, I hadn't killed 엄마, he'd insist. He'd talk, again, of the harsh past. Kin split; this land, ripped apart. Invaded. Pillaged. In just the 1950s, more U.S. shells falling in Korea than in all of the Pacific through the 1940s. Spilt life fed this soil. I was forged in ash. It helped explain this past, the sole hostile spirit. It lent people hope to think, Oh, if I do this, I'll escape fresh pain. It's nothing but a tale.

34.

I said no. Pah, did you think I hoped to be his wife? Like I said, not a life worth having. Still, I kept up the act. I told High-hat that, if we fled, we'd die starving. I'm just a simple village girl, I said. I don't mind hardship. But I'd reject letting High-hat live with such pain. If I stayed, though, I'd be left open to his father's rage.

High-hat had a shit fit, railing at his father's parting words. Such evil things he'd said. I, his bride, had to be avenged. So, I told High-hat I had an idea. I might die, if I didn't run. Spirits loved at will. I helped High-hat scale the pine, its bark rough. Petal skin, I thought. Soft, upright child. She'd live a long time. Let it be a gentle life. High-hat and I jumped.

I won't quit this world, I figured. No, I'd died with things to do. I was right, as usual. High-hat's father wailing, I rolled in his tears. Oh, he tore his fine silk to rags. Next, I'd zip up the walls. I'd howl at the light. I leapt, riding the wind.

35

On a plane, Philip and I left Seoul. I thought of 아버지, living alone. I'd asked if, staying behind, I might be useful. No, he had a life in Seoul, his job. I should get back; he'd visit.

•

I slept awhile, the first night home. I woke, gasping. Philip had gone out. He'd be right back, his note said. I had to decide what I was going to do: Philip, for one. Lidija, too. Irate spirit. Nigel's photos; the hospital oath. I got up to sit in the kitchen, on cold tiles. I listed objects lining the wall. Pickled figs, kettle, pied salt mill. Pothos, olive oil. Jade plant, lime basil. I kept going until the panic lulled. Philip came back with bags, as well as a pot of pignoli juk from Hiju. Sahaj had also left a fruit basket while I slept. Did I want Philip to heat the juk? Or he—

"How'd they all find out?"

"I told Hiju," Philip said, his face open, soft. "I think he up-dated the others. Jin, did I fuck up, telling Hiju?"

In New York, the first place we'd shared, a birch lived in front of the building. It was Philip who caught sight of the ori-ole's nest in the birch, with its tight, pink bouquet of nestlings' mouths. If the wind was high, this refuge brushed the sill. But one night, as we read, my head lying in Philip's lap, I heard shrill chirping. Oriole nestlings, tufts of down, had fallen on the sill. Outside, the branch testified to a lethal fight, its nest ripped, plumes snarled in twigs. Infant birds bled, the bodies mangled.

Philip, frantic, called a wild-bird refuge, a hospital. But nothing could help. Even while Philip made his calls, the chirps quieted. In the end, I killed the birds. I sliced nestling heads with a chef's knife. High, frenzied chirps; the sharp hush. I'd wept, furious I'd hoped to avoid inflicting pain.

"No, you did the right thing," I said. I lifted the lid on Hiju's juk. Still hot, rich with pignoli. I tried a liquid bite, then kept eating.

●

I went to St. George's, a church. On walks, I'd often pass the building, its finial gold spires glinting, a tall sign hailing the dragon-slaying icon. For a while, he'd lost his high position.

Not quite a full saint, the Pope had said. More of a legend, his hero's exploits alleged. Milk rilling, prolific, out of his lopped head; a riot of foliage, virid fibrils coiling from the planks upon which he'd bled. People who'd died hurtling to life, roaring to be baptized. Idols spalled; pagan hordes, jubilant, turning to the Lord.

It's the gist of faith's orphic pledge: loss repaid. Life going on. I held 엄마's note; I kept it intact. I sat in the echoing church, then left. I put the note in my studio desk. If 엄마 still had words to pass along, she hadn't quite died.

·

Dear Lord, I thought that, if I lost You, I'd have to stop living. I kept going, in part, to still have the hope of finding You again. It's absurd; Lord, it makes me laugh. But if, in the house of logic, my dead will not exist, I'm obliged to step outside. O Lord, each photo is for You. I spill light. I leak worship, and Lord, if I get it right, will You come back?

·

Not long ago, Philip walked in the studio while I cried. I'd read a profile of the Polish artist staging wish-filling photos of ill, dying kids. Girl as witch; a child, the lion king. One kid, afraid of dying, had a plan. He'd join his parents in a fixed spot, just at the afterlife's gates. Until his parents died, he'd wait in that place.

"Oh, I'm glad," Philip said, with a sigh. He'd put his head next to mine. "It's a plan."

I laughed, startled. "It is?"

"It's a plan, so his parents will find him," Philip said, going in the kitchen.

*

I woke that night half-drunk from wine. Still tasting the bold, stale tang of spoiled fruit, I let the bath tap open. But darting up, I raced out; naked, I got the laptop from my handbag. For the first time, I split in piles the self-portraits I'd kept: yes, no. Each yes had to ring loud, bright. It had to be full, a hallelujah.

I had forty photos in the pile of yes, all of which I sent to Chi. "None of it's for Nigel," I told him. "I'm trying out ideas." Plus, I had editing to do, photos to add; I'd love Chi's opinion. One, from Marin, depicted Lidija's thigh flush against my leg. It was just Chi. I'd edit out Lidija. Nothing was final. I'd explain; I'd take the photos back. Now, I'd wash, I thought. But I'd failed to twist the spigot closed. It was hot, the walls slick, paint rising. Spirals of mist. Prodigal, I felt the paint welts. Once, I'd figured this world's glyphs to be divine, each jot part of His design. It's a past life, but O Lord, I will still rejoice.

•

I held the phone as it jerked. "Chi?" I asked. I'd just woken up; he'd left calls.

"You."

"Chi, tell me what you think."

"It's thrilling, Jin. I don't have to tell you this. But what's going to Nigel?"

I told Chi I had to go. He asked if I was fucking kidding. I hung up. High gusts; the flap of wings, throat rasping. Panic surging, I groped the phone. I sent Lidija a line, asking that we talk.

•

I'd curled on the tiles again. Listing plants, I heard light steps rattling the porch. Nhi had told Philip she'd drop off Helen's tsebhi. It was hot enough that, after a while, I went out. I had no tsebhi pan, though. On the porch wall: a sign, a public bill. In paint, siren-red. It still hadn't set, the drip paint fluid. I toed liquid. *Heretic*, it said. I should be afraid, I thought. But rage licked up from paint, limbs firing. It dispelled all panic; I inhaled, in full.

•

I was in bed that night, with Philip, when Lidija called. "Jin, I'm in a hotel."

Philip, reading, lifted his head. I'd wiped much of the red paint, not all. I'd told him, at last, about hostile mail, the Baptist artist ban. I'd hoped to ignore it, I'd said. Philip had replied, calm, that we'd surveil the porch. Quelling his disquiet, again, I thought. His wife, upset; Philip, equable, in this forced role. "It's Lidija," I said, to Philip.

"I, what hotel?" I asked Lidija, from the studio.

"No, I'm going first. Seoul?"

I'd had to take a last-minute trip, I said. I didn't explain. In Lidija's world, I had both parents, living. It spun past, this parallel life, as though it might still exist. "But I'm home again. Lidija, what's this hotel?"

"I'm also taking a trip," Lidija said, full laugh tolling. "No, bring him back. It has to be a pail, large. Not just the ice."

"Ice?"

"People are here. Jin, I'm—"

I heard rustling; the call died.

•

Philip had left out a cup of puerh. I rinsed his glass. Once, with Philip in Beijing, I'd kept a cup of his tea, along with its puerh silt. In case, I'd thought. If, oh, a plane crashed. It might be a last object still having a trace, this final relic, of Philip. His spit, flaked bits of lip. Until I had Philip home again, I didn't wash his cup.

•

I had to stop lying. On the night after Lidija's call, I led Philip to sit. "In there," I said, giving him the laptop.

"Jin, what is this?"

"Philip, please, first look at it."

He did, then he put the laptop down. "Is this Lidija?"

"It is."

"Did you fuck Lidija?"

I nodded.

"Is the—"

"It's not an excuse, Philip, but I tried. I asked."

"I don't like hurting you. Is that so fucking bad?"

"No."

"I'd have kept trying, if you'd said."

"I did tell you. But you said that, if I'd wait, you'd learn—"

"If I—"

"It was so hard to ask, Philip, then—"

"Oh, I'm the one at fault?"

"No. It's just, I couldn't push. I still can't."

"If a friend had shown me this shit, I'd have thought it false."

Philip jumped up. He said I had to explain. No, he'd get out; Philip fled.

36.

Quit of the earth's pull, I glided. I filched jades, hurling ink pots. Upside-down, I'd hiss. I leapt at noble jerks. I'd laugh at each prig who'd piss his silk baji. Oh, what of High-hat? His spirit moped along. Last I heard, he might have left this world. Listen, I don't give a shit. I pitched inlaid jars. I slit bojagi.

But hijinks aside, I didn't forget the shaman's words. In life, we'd be split. Spot-on bitch. I'd thought it all out. I'd be tip-top, in spirit form, at helping. In hard times, while the rich starved, I pilfered. I relied on magpies to drop jewel spoils in her jeogori. If foreign shitbags got close to the walls, I'd shriek; they'd run. Soldiers, pah. People said a raging ghost lived in the place. I didn't, but I kept the house safe.

37.

I sat while the sun, falling, bled into night. It was light out again; the bell rang. Philip, I thought, lunging up. It was Elise, holding a large pot. "I bring gifts," she said. Nudging me aside with her hip, she bustled in. Elise ignited the pilot light. It was Hiju's pignoli juk, a fresh batch. Philip had asked Hiju where he might get this kind of juk. It was all I'd eat, he'd said. She'd heat it up. "Hiju added a bottle of soju. It pairs with the juk."

I sat on the tiles, legs failing.

"Oh, Jin," Elise said. "She loved you so much."

"It's not just that. It is, but—"

•

Elise filled the kettle while I spoke of Philip, Lidija, the deli, a night in Marin. "I've tried finding this wish, for having a child.

If I had the urge, well. But all I find, in its place, is this pure, solid refusal. I can't give in. I'd resent Philip, along with the child. So, I hoped he'd—oh, Christ. Elise, I hoped he'd change his mind."

She held out a hot cup, then slid to the tiles. "Hiju fucked a physicist, right after Lionel's birth."

"Hiju did *what*?"

"She's from Paris. It was one night." I flailed, upset. I'd lost the right to wrath, a loyal friend's railing. Hiju injured a person I loved; so had I.

"I did think of fucking Hiju's friend's wife," Elise said, flashing a smile. "She kept flirting. Hiju's close friend, who used to work in his Chicago lab. Might as well begin a fire in each part of Hiju's life, I figured. I didn't think we'd get through it, for a while. But I told Hiju he gets this big misstep. Hiju's used his. I still might. I think Hiju felt he'd lost a slice of the person he thought he'd be. Jin, is Philip talking, at all, of his role in having this child?"

"Philip said he'd be the child's first parent. But he'd be gone, at his job. I'd give birth, then I'd be home."

"Is he open to adopting?"

"I didn't—"

"It's not simple. But, like fostering, it's a path. Oh, hiring live-in help. Hiju's said it's what people often do, in Korea, hiring aid, live-in help, for a month. Months, plural. Is Philip up on all this?"

"No, but—"

"Hiju did find a person to fill this role, for Shiloh. But with Hiju's parents living in Vallejo, I said let's not. I can't tell you, Jin, how much it helps. Hiju's parents, willing to be with the kids. Not just willing. Imploring. In Chicago, Hiju and I had just us. Philip often travels, for his job. Is he telling you how he'd adjust that portion of his life?"

"No."

"Sybil, a friend. She's a pianist, who—"

"Right, Sybil."

"Ishaq, Sybil's husband, also didn't want a child. But then, Ishaq did. Sybil refused. It's a roving life, with Sybil often in, I have no idea, Berlin. Leipzig. He's the first parent, though. If he fails, they'll split. Ishaq will have the kid full-time. It's all in writing, Jin. Ishaq's parents live in town. Siblings. Is Philip doing anything like this?"

I'd set down the cup; I held my head. "No. But he'd adopt, I think. I did put off talking. I told Philip to wait, until the fall. He might be an expert, at this point, on kids."

"Do you think he is?"

"Well," I said. "No."

"Jin," Elise said. "I love Philip. I do. Still, it's his job, sorting this out. Lionel's wild about playing with his shit. Crib slats, his legs, he's flinging shit. Lionel, first-born child, is the Irene Chou of shit paint. No, it's all right. You can laugh.

It cracks up Lionel, too. But Jin, I miss Lionel while he's taking a nap. I'll stand at his crib, just crying. I itch to bring a third child to life. I won't do it, but I'm craving a passel. Six kids. It helps, a little, as I'm wiping fresh shit from the walls, that I'd pick this again. Shit paint and all. I think nothing will make this child possible for you. But Philip isn't giving this a lot of thought. It's a mother's job. Is that his logic? No."

Rising, she lifted the juk pot lid. She got a ladle from where it hung.

"So, lying to Philip. Not ideal; still, it isn't all you. But photos, with Lidija. Jin, you hid this part."

·

Elise and I spoke, candid, at length. But, I said, she also had images, up to Shiloh's arrival. It might still be useful, perhaps. I stared, waiting, at pignoli juk, oil gilding the rice. She chortled; I jolted back, rice sloshing.

"No, it's just that, Jin, it's also hard asking you how it's going. I'm taking photos. Post-birth images. I kept it quiet until the project felt less rough. I'll finish, before long. So, I'm using the old images, after all."

I'd put down the juk as I wiped the spill with a rag, which let me jump at Elise. She fell. Oh, so I'd hid photos. I flicked the rag, its clean end, at Elise. She had image again.

•

Elise left; after a while, the phone flared. It was Philip, a line. "I broke a pact first," he said.

I yelped. Elated, I thought, but no, I wailed. It split, then, part of the bind. He'd forgive the lies; images, Lidija. But Philip, he'd still want a child. He'd go on living with this abiding, crucial lack. If I stayed with him, I laid a curse upon us both. Philip hoped I'd give him what he desired; I won't. Others, though, will.

•

But I'd also just rinsed a plate. I held the sink, wailing. In the glass ahead, faint, I had an image. Its flitting light. Pulled-open, gaping mouth. Its torque, the weft. Falling lines. I wept; I also sidled out of the pain, alert. It was a novel sight, this anguish. I had to get a photo. I ran to my bag.

•

Lidija had gone to Milan. Neil gave the ballet funding. No one's finding out, he'd said. But if people did, she'd still prefer it to Josip, Thijs. Lidija tried out, the leg holding strong. Invited to join, she'd said yes. "I'll have a big place. Jin, live with me, in Milan. Will you?"

"In Milan," I said, addled. I sat on a porch step.

"It'd be ours."

"Neil will be with you?"

"Not often."

"So, you're asking that I live in Milan, but with Neil show-ing up."

"I'd go to a hotel," Lidija said. "Jin, you're living with Philip."

"If the ballet you're staging—"

"It's not a real hope."

I thought of the rallied ghost. "Lidija, Neil—"

"I'd do it again. Jin, I'm dancing. Neil helps."

"But if Josip, with Neil—"

"I can't prove it. Jin, you had help, Philip, all along. I'm short on help, but I have Neil. It's top-flight ballet. Of all—"

"Lidija, I'd hide. I can't be in public with you. Is that right?"

Silent, a silk-robed kisaeng lolled against the wall. I pictured the life Lidija offered. Being Lidija's secret; eluding prying. I felt the still-healing burn, its pain dull. Not quite solicited, like the night I was choked. I didn't forbid the ballet plan. None of this being Lidija's fault: I might have replied with a no. But I'd told Lidija the old Han tale had to be private, a limit she'd ig-nored. She did push. I had trouble refusing Lidija. Nights, I'd wait for Lidija to get home. Neil would call. She'd go to him. I had just begun hiding less. In Milan, I'd sit captive, building the cage.

"I'm glad you'll be dancing ballet," I said. "I can't live with you, though."

"Jin—"

•

I called Chi. I hoped to exhibit the photos I'd staged. But after finding a shaman, I said. One who'd call forth a spirit. It was hard to explain. I'd had a ghost inspire the art. She, this spirit, might not wish to talk. I'd be lying, with each image, if I hadn't tried. It might not be real, but I'd ask for the spirit's help. So, I had nothing to give Nigel. I had a friend, though, Elise Liu. She had photos fitting Nigel's idea. Elise didn't exhibit much, yet. Still, I'd call this friend a genius. Chi might, too. If he did, could Nigel, perhaps, be open to taking Elise's work, instead?

•

I sat on the front porch, its top step. Singed air burned again, but I'd watch for Philip. I'd explain, if I could. I rolled a felled, rotting apple from the step. One from, I thought, Sahaj's fruit basket. It left a wet spot. Philip, in Noxhurst, had taken me apple-picking. It was the fall we'd started dating; boughs dangled partial globes of apple-sculpted ice. Ghost apples, Philip said. Fruit slipped, as pulp, through frozen hulls. Ice held the apples' shape.

I still had photos I'd shot with Philip, in the orchard. I'd kept the late sun's path of gold, showing a life ahead. Philip can tell which apple each bough will yield. It turns into a game. I point; he'll call its name. Empire. Lodi. Spigold. Pippin. I pick fruit he'll put in a basket. Philip's hands cold, he adjusts the piles. It's part of what I'll love in Philip, his deft, able tending of the harvest. No fruit will be left bruised.

I'll love him. It isn't going to be enough. "Philip," I call. It's him, palm lifting. Philip, almost home.

38.

THE KISAENG'S STORY, AS TOLD TO JIN HAN

But such pride, acting like I'd punish you Hans for talking. Listen, I don't give a dog's shit what you people do. Oh, I played tricks. It's just that, like I said, I don't forget.

Go tell people what I did. Sing of this gifted kisaeng's exploits! Pah, I'm not still here for dipshit Hans. I'm patient. I had a single hope. I tallied the length of time she'd live.

39.

June again, living in New York. I had, with Chi, a follow-up solo opening. On this soft, hot night, thick with a flashing past, I'd walk. In the afterlife I won't find, I'll sit with all the people I've lost, and we'll laugh at the prodigals we used to be. Once, long ago, we split apart. No such thing will happen again.

I idled at the light, until I kept going.

40.

THE KISAENG'S STORY, AS TOLD TO JIN HAN

No, I didn't find my friend. But I will. I float, calling. I kick the flaking shale. I nudge high cattails; I part trailing fronds. If she's tangled in grass, I'll wed its soil. I'll ravel lush tendrils along hers. I'll push up, frothing with life. Sprigs will fill out, rising in fresh, solid boughs.

She and I, we'll get tall. Limbs joined, burst into the light.

Acknowledgments

With love and gratitude to my agent, Ellen Levine, along with Ana Ban, Audrey Crooks, Miles Temel, and Martha Wydysh;

to my editor, Laura Perciasepe, and publicist, Glory Anne Plata, as well as the many others at Riverhead and Penguin Random House who helped make this book possible, including Afarin Allabakhshizadeh, Robert Belmont, Carla Benton, Brian Contine, Nora Alice Demick, Lexie Farabaugh, Sydney Fowler, John Francisconi, Ashley Garland, Geoffrey Kloske, Hannah Lopez, Jynne Dilling Martin, Randee Marullo, Caitlin Noonan, Wendy Pearl, Drew Schnoebelen, Ariel So, Melissa Solis, and Claire Vaccaro;

to my film and television agents, Addison Duffy and Jasmine Lake;

to the Tuesday Agency, and Ariel Lewiton, Kevin Mills, Trinity Ray, and Rachel Yoder;

to Jesse Dittmar, Jacqueline McDonald, Vi-An Nguyen, and Eric Traore;

to the Bread Loaf Writers' Conference, MacDowell, Scripps College, Stanford University, Tin House Workshop, University of San Francisco, and Yaddo;

to booksellers and librarians, for lighting a path;

to Andrew Sean Greer, Raven Leilani, Madeline Miller, Bryan Washington, and C Pam Zhang, for the generosity of early words of support;

to Lauren Markham and Ingrid Rojas Contreras, for vital, abiding kinship;

to Rabih Alameddine, Indira Allegra, Jennifer Baker, Jeremiah Barber, Bahar Behbahani, Elaine Castillo, Alexander Chee, Kirstin Chen, Susan Choi, Nicole Chung, Harriet Clark, Natalie Diaz, Isaac Fitzgerald, Garth Greenwell, Lauren Groff, Anisse Gross, Anthony Ha, Elliott Holt, Hong Hong, Chloe Honum, Vanessa Hua, Mira Jacob, Rachel Khong, Lydia Kiesling, Alice Sola Kim, Crystal Hana Kim, Katie Kitamura, Lisa Ko, Chang-rae Lee, Krys Lee, Min Jin Lee, Yiyun Li, Michael David Lukas, Karan Mahajan, Caille Millner, Nayomi Munaweera, Celeste Ng, Beth Nguyen, Anna North, Antoinette Nwandu, Jenny Odell, Aimee Phan, Camille Rankine, Enrico Rotelli, Margaret Wilkerson Sexton, M. A. Taft-McPhee, Nafissa Thompson-Spires, Tony Tulathimutte, Asmin Tulpule, Laura van den Berg, Vauhini Vara, Oscar Villalon, Ayelet Waldman, Esmé Weijun

Wang, Andi Winnette, Colin Winnette, Annie Julia Wyman, Emily Jungmin Yoon, Lidia Yuknavitch, and Jenny Zhang, whose crucial friendship, example, or both helped this book go on;

to Kyra Hegewald, Rachel Howard, Juliana Jensen, Jonathan David Jordan, Michael Montgomery, Nicia Moura, Benedict Nguyen, Mimi Plumb, Peter Prato, Jessica Richman, and Karl Soehnlein, for large gifts of time and wisdom;

to Callum Angus, Vanessa Clark, Kim Fu, Roxane Gay, Cara Hoffman, Zeyn Joukhadar, Zachary Knoll, Chris Kraus, Carmen Maria Machado, Peter Mountford, Larissa Pham, and Brandon Taylor, for *Kink* camaraderie;

to Periplus, and to Brandon Choi, Goeun Park, and Krys Shin;

to Michael Cunningham, first mentor;

to André Aciman, Charles Baxter, Amy Bloom, Peter Ho Davies, Stacey D'Erasmo, Joshua Henkin, Jennifer Kennedy, Ernesto Mestre, Jenny Offill, Christine Schutt, Catherine Texier, and Katharine Weber, my teachers;

to Clara Kwon and Young Kwon, as well as Carl Dawson, Lynn Dawson, Byung Rim Kwon, Christine Ji Min Kwon, Ella Kwon, John Okeun Kwon, Michael Kwon, Tae Ryong Kwon, Agnes Shin, and Chang Ho Shin, always;

to M., at whose side no afterlife will be enough.

Notes

30 **It can be malign, hitched as it is to bad, old ideas:** Sigmund Freud, in 1920, called sadomasochism the "most significant of all perversions." Until 2013, varieties of kink were classified as markers of mental illness in the *Diagnostic and Statistical Manual of Mental Disorders*, or the *DSM*. By some measures, kinky people amount to at least forty percent of the population.

31 **Ill-used, and glad of it:** In 1875, the Page Act stopped the immigration of Chinese women on the stated pretext that they were "immoral." It was the first federal border-closing law in the U.S.

39 **Noted sijos, kisaengs' poems, had survived:** Examples of kisaeng poets whose work is studied include Hwang Jini, Keju, and Songi.

68 **Dying lasted months, a terrible death:** In 1863, Emma Livry died of a gas-lamp fire.

117 **I didn't like the idea of facing Julian:** Yu Guan Soon formed a student resistance group to protest the Japanese occupation of Korea, and played a significant role in organizing a march that began on March 1, 1919. Two million people, a tenth of Korea's population, protested.

Imprisoned and tortured for her political activities, Yu died before turning eighteen years old.

135 **It goes on swilling:** Quotation from Franz Kafka: "How wonderful that is, isn't it? The lilac—dying, it drinks, goes on swilling."

148 **Had Lidija tried this kind of ballet:** *En Puntas* by Javier Pérez, at the Teatre Municipal de Girona, in Spain, in 2013, performed by dancer Amélie Segarra.